Henry Cecil was the pseudony
Leon. He was born in Norwood Green Rectory, near
London, England in 1902. He studied at Cambridge
where he edited an undergraduate magazine and wrote a
Footlights May Week production. Called to the bar in
1923, he served with the British Army during the Second
World War. While in the Middle East with his battalion he
used to entertain the troops with a serial story each
evening. This formed the basis of his first book, *Full Circle*.
He was appointed a County Court Judge in 1949 and held
that position until 1967. The law and the circumstances
which surround it were the source of his many novels,
plays, and short stories. His books are works of great
comic genius with unpredictable twists of plot which
highlight the often absurd workings of the English legal
system. He died in 1976.

BY THE SAME AUTHOR
ALL PUBLISHED BY HOUSE OF STRATUS

BRIEF TALES
FROM THE BENCH

by

Henry Cecil

HOUSE OF
STRATUS

This edition published in 2000 by House of Stratus, an imprint of
Stratus Holdings plc, 24c Old Burlington Street, London, W1X 1RL, UK.

www.houseofstratus.com

Typeset, printed and bound by House of Stratus.

A catalogue record for this book is available from the British Library.

ISBN 1-84232-042-4

Contents

Introduction

As a County Court judge for eighteen years I tried many thousands of cases. Half of the cases in this book are based, or partly based, on actual experience, while half are pure fiction. I have stated in an appendix at the end of the book which is which. In the cases which have a factual basis I have not disclosed the true identity of the parties concerned.

The stories were originally broadcast by the BBC on radio in the form of half-hour plays, and Mr Andrew Cruickshank played the leading part. None of them has been published previously except 'Chef's Special', which appeared in *Argosy*.

CHAPTER ONE

Contempt of Court

Most people in every walk of life have power and sometimes abuse it. Judges in their own courts have very considerable power. A judge may fine or send to prison anyone who improperly interrupts the proceedings. Only Parliament has a similar power. In order that the business of a court may be properly carried on, it is necessary for a judge to have this power. But it is just as important that he should not abuse it. It is very doubtful if today any judges abuse their power to fine or imprison for contempt of court. But undoubtedly from time to time judges do abuse their power by saying things which are hurtful to somebody and unnecessary for the purposes of the case. Judges are after all only human beings and must from time to time fail in the proper discharge of their duties. But a judge should at all times be on his guard against making this type of error.

People are so very polite, not to say obsequious, to judges that there is a danger that a judge may think that he is just as important out of court as he is in court, when in fact he is not. It is the office which is important, not the man. This is easy to state, but not always so easy, for an average person like myself, to remember.

1

One day I was driving towards my court and had reached one of the back streets three or four hundred yards away from the court building. A coalman was delivering coal, and, owing to an unattended parked car, there just wasn't room enough for my car to get between that car and the coal lorry. So I stopped and got out and went up to the coalman.

'Would you mind moving your lorry a foot or so, so that I can get through?'

'I will when I've finished,' said the coalman.

'How long will that be?' I asked.

'You'll see,' he replied.

'I'd be awfully grateful,' I said, 'if you could move it now.'

'I told you I'd move it when I'd finished,' said the man.

As it was close on time for the court to begin and I didn't want to be late, I said: 'As a matter of fact I happen to be the judge of the Willesden County Court which is just round the corner, and there are a lot of people waiting for me to try their cases. If I can't go through now, I shall be late.'

'You'll be late then,' said the coalman, and went on delivering his coal.

There was nothing left for me to do but to wait as patiently as possible in my car. After five or ten minutes the man finished his delivery and went to his cab and stood by it. Then very slowly he extracted a packet of cigarettes from his pocket. Very slowly he took a cigarette out of the packet, and then replaced it in his pocket. Then he searched for a match and, taking far more time than was necessary, lighted the cigarette. Still standing on the ground, he took several puffs, and then very slowly clambered into the lorry. He then arranged himself preparatory to driving, took a few more puffs at his cigarette, and then finally started the engine. He waited for about a quarter of a minute and finally drove towards me. As his cab drew level with me, he leaned out and said: 'Are you in a hurry, mate?'

So far, this was a case of a coalman abusing his power, not a judge. As soon as I could, I drove to court and got on with my work. But during an adjournment I turned up the County Courts Act, and saw, as I had suspected was the case, that anyone who insulted the judge going to or coming from court, was liable to be imprisoned for one month, or to pay a fine of ten pounds.

Now, obviously, to be guilty of that contempt, you must know that the person whom you insult is a judge. But I had told the coalman that I was the judge, and there was no earthly reason why he should have disbelieved me. Indeed, had he been doubtful about my identification, he could have asked me for some proof of it, and I had documents on me which would have satisfied anybody. So I told the registrar to give notice to the coalman, whose employer's name I had taken, to attend court on a particular day to show cause why he should not be dealt with for contempt of court.

When the bailiff of the court delivered this document to the coalman, whose name was Albert Smith, naturally the man was rather worried about it. The bailiff advised him to go and consult a solicitor. Mr Smith very wisely took the bailiff's advice and consulted a Mr Tewkesbury.

Mr Tewkesbury, I'm glad to say, was by no means a typical solicitor. There are a few bad sheep in every fold, and I'm afraid that he was one of them.

Naturally I cannot vouch for what happened in Mr Tewkesbury's office, but I don't think that I should be far wrong if I described the scene as follows.

When Mr Smith arrived at his office, Mr Tewkesbury was sleeping off the effects of the last bottle of whisky which he'd had.

'Mr Tewkesbury,' said Bella, his typist, secretary and general maid-of-all-work, 'Mr Tewkesbury, there's a customer.'

Mr Tewkesbury woke up slowly.

'Client, girl,' he said.

'What's the difference, Mr Tewkesbury?'

'Well,' said Mr Tewkesbury, 'greengrocers have customers, solicitors have clients.'

'But why, Mr Tewkesbury?'

'I'll tell you another time. Now what did you want to wake me up for?'

'There's a client.'

'Has he an appointment?'

'No, Mr Tewkesbury.'

'Then he can wait a bit. He mustn't think I've nothing else to do. Where's that bottle I told you to get?'

'Oh, Mr Tewkesbury,' said Bella, 'I thought – I thought you'd be better without it.'

'How old are you, girl?' said Mr Tewkesbury.

'I'm twenty-one.' And then she added, defensively: 'nearly twenty-two.'

'Well,' said Mr Tewkesbury, 'you're not old enough to be my father or my mother yet, are you?'

'No, Mr Tewkesbury.'

'Well,' said Mr Tewkesbury, 'no doubt you meant it for good. But let me tell you, girl, that my best work is done when pickled.'

'You don't say, Mr Tewkesbury,' said Bella.

'But I do say. Did you hear me in court in the Robinson case?'

'No, I didn't.'

'Well, I'm glad,' said Mr Tewkesbury. 'I was stone cold sober. Quite unfit to be in charge of any case. Now tell me, girl, how long have you been with me?'

'Two weeks, Mr Tewkesbury.'

'As long as that? Well done. What's your real name, girl?'

'Bella, Mr Tewkesbury.'

'D'you mind me calling you "girl"?'

'I don't mind what you call me, Mr Tewkesbury, so long as you don't call me late for dinner.'

'Well, well, well,' said Mr Tewkesbury. 'Who taught you that?'

'My auntie used to say that,' said Bella.

'Good gracious,' said Mr Tewkesbury. 'I first heard it from my grandmother. I didn't know anybody knew it now. How would you like to have dinner with me, girl?'

'Don't you think you ought to see Mr Smith?' said Bella.

'And who might he be?'

'The client, Mr Tewkesbury.'

'Not much of a name, Smith,' said Mr Tewkesbury ruminatively. 'You may not believe it, girl, but I've had double-barrels coming to this office.'

'I can quite believe it, Mr Tewkesbury,' said Bella.

'Dukes, captains of industry, no prime ministers yet, but several cabinet ministers.'

'But what's wrong with "Smith" Mr Tewkesbury? After all, Mr Brown's name is only Mr Brown.'

'That's a profound thought, girl,' said Mr Tewkesbury. 'I must remember that. That should take the double-barrels down a bit. Mr Brown's name, I shall say, is only Mr Brown. And what does Mr Smith do?'

'He says he's a coalman,' said Bella.

'Ah,' said Mr Tewkesbury, 'he's come anonymously. It's really Lord Robens. Show him in at once, girl. I never keep peers of the realm waiting.'

'Very good, sir,' said Bella.

Bella went out and brought Mr Smith in.

'Pray sit down, my lord,' said Mr Tewkesbury.

'Fanks,' said Mr Smith.

'What did you say?' asked Mr Tewkesbury.

'I said "Fanks",' repeated Mr Smith.

'Oh,' said Mr Tewkesbury. 'Then you're not Lord Robens?'

'Not wot?'

'Never mind,' said Mr Tewkesbury. 'What can I do for you?'

So Mr Smith showed Mr Tewkesbury the notice which he had received from the court.

'You'd like me to appear for you?'

'Yes,' said Mr Smith.

'Give me the diary, Miss Bell, please,' said Mr Tewkesbury. 'Let me see. I have two cases in the High Court on that day, and a consultation with Sir Mark Burnham. A couple of little things in the Magistrates' Court, and a few conferences. Yes, I think I shall be able to manage that all right, Mr Smith. The fee will be ten guineas.'

'That's coming it a bit,' said Mr Smith.

'The trouble is,' said Mr Tewkesbury, 'that the judge might come it a bit more. You've never been to prison before, I take it?'

'Course not.'

'Well, I should have thought it was worth ten guineas to stay out of it.'

Well, whether it happened like that or not, I don't know. But I do know that, when the case was called on, Mr Tewkesbury was appearing for Mr Smith. He was not particularly sober, but he was able to enunciate clearly, perhaps even rather more clearly than when sober. The first thing he did when the case was called on was to get up and say: 'I object, your honour.'

I asked him to what he objected.

'Your honour,' said Mr Tewkesbury, 'may I say that I have always had the greatest respect, not to say affection, for your honour?'

'No,' I said, 'Mr Tewkesbury, you may not. It has nothing to do with the case.'

'I am loath to disagree with your honour,' said Mr Tewkesbury. 'And it ill becomes one in my lowly position to contradict your honour. Rome wasn't built in a day, your honour. *Per ardua ad astra.*'

'Mr Tewkesbury,' I said, perhaps a little testily, 'will you kindly come to the point.'

'I was soaring to it, your honour,' said Mr Tewkesbury. 'I'd reached the point where I'd assured your honour that I held your honour in great respect, not to say affection.'

'And I've reached the point,' I said, 'where I'm not going to stand any more of this. If you have an objection to make, kindly make it. What do you object to?'

'I object,' said Mr Tewkesbury, 'with the greatest humility and the utmost respect – I object to your honour.'

'I beg your pardon?' I asked.

'It is for me to beg yours, your honour,' said Mr Tewkesbury.

'You mean you object to me?' I said. 'You object to my trying the case?'

'Your honour,' said Mr Tewkesbury, 'as usual you have my point almost before I've made it.'

'What are the grounds for your objection?' I asked.

'There's nothing personal in it, your honour,' said Mr Tewkesbury.

'I dare say not,' I said, 'but what are your grounds?'

'Well,' said Mr Tewkesbury, 'your honour, to put it shortly, and again assuring your honour of the deep respect in which I hold your honour – indeed in which I hold all Her Majesty's judges – and making it clear that in saying what I am, I have no intention whatever – '

'Mr Tewkesbury,' I interrupted, 'you said you were going to put it shortly. Kindly do so.'

'Well,' said Mr Tewkesbury, 'in a word, your honour, no, it can't be done in one word. Does your honour wish to know the exact number of words?'

'So long as there aren't too many,' I said, 'I don't mind how many there are.'

'Your honour is very gracious,' said Mr Tewkesbury.

'Mr Tewkesbury,' I said, 'if you don't tell me within the next half minute what your objection is, I shall be anything but gracious.'

'Your honour,' said Mr Tewkesbury, 'is very kind. Well, your honour, my objection in a word, no, not in a word, but shall we say in a – in a nutshell is this. It's ten words as a matter of fact. That's not too many, I hope?'

'Go on, please.'

'With the ten words, your honour?'

'Yes.'

'Well, your honour, the ten words. I think they're ten, your honour, but I might have counted wrong. Your honour will forgive me if I have. The ten words are "no one should be a judge in his own cause".'

I realised at once that, although Mr Tewkesbury's method of putting it could hardly be described as highly satisfactory, there was a good deal to be said for his submission. If a man insults a judge in open court, everyone can see that justice is done if he's punished for that offence. But when the offence, if any, is committed where the public cannot see it, it doesn't seem right that the judge who complains about it, should try the case himself.

'I think you're right, Mr Tewkesbury,' I said. 'I'll adjourn the case for another judge to deal with it. Will next Monday suit you and your client?'

It soon became very plain that neither next Monday nor any other day suited Mr Smith. He plainly wanted the case heard there and then. I could see his point of view. He didn't want it hanging over his head. After a few minutes' discussion with Mr Tewkesbury, he could not restrain himself any longer.

'I want to know what's going to happen,' he said out loud. 'My missus is all over the place about it. I've come here today to have it dealt with, and it's not fair to make me come another day.'

Mr Tewkesbury then informed me that his client would be perfectly happy for me to deal with the matter. But I was not prepared to do so. I did not know what the man was going to say. For all I knew he would tell a completely different story from mine. I couldn't say that I'd known myself from a very early age, and that I was prepared to accept everything that I said. It was my own cause. I could not be a judge in it myself. On the other hand, it would be very hard on Mr Smith to be kept in suspense. Then I had an idea. I accordingly suggested that the Lord Chancellor might be asked to appoint a deputy-judge from one of the barristers who were at the court at the moment. Mr Tewkesbury agreed, and in consequence, Mr Benton, a barrister of considerable experience, was appointed a deputy-judge for the express purpose of trying this matter of contempt of court.

The problem then arose as to how the case was to be tried. None of us could see any alternative to my going into the witness box as an ordinary witness. How else could justice be done and be seen to be done? I had never seen or heard of a contempt case being dealt with in that manner before, but I did not see how it could be properly dealt with otherwise. If Mr Smith's evidence was to be heard on oath, why shouldn't mine also? If he was to be cross-examined, why shouldn't I be cross-examined?

So the consequence was that Mr Benton took my place on the bench, and I went into the witness box. I stated on oath what had happened. And then I was cross-examined by Mr Tewkesbury. First of all, however, he addressed the deputy-judge.

'Your honour, what shall I call his honour, your honour?'

'What d'you mean?' asked the deputy-judge.

'Well,' said Mr Tewkesbury, 'if I say "your honour" you will think I'm talking to you. If I don't say anything at all, he'll think I'm being disrespectful.'

'As far as I'm concerned, your honour,' I said, 'Mr Tewkesbury need call me nothing at all.'

'Thank you, your honour,' said the deputy-judge.

'Not at all, your honour,' said I.

But Mr Tewkesbury had the last word.

'I thank both your honours,' he said.

Then he actually got on with the job of cross-examining me.

'Your complaint is,' he asked, 'that my client wouldn't move his lorry before he'd finished delivering the coal?'

'Not quite that,' I said, 'but that in refusing to move it he behaved in a deliberately insulting manner after I'd told him I was the judge of the court.'

'Let's see how he behaved,' said Mr Tewkesbury. 'You say he took a packet of cigarettes out of his pocket and did it very slowly. Are you able to say that he didn't find the packet tangled up with string or sticking plaster in his pocket?'

'I didn't think he had any difficulty,' I said, 'but I can't say for certain.'

'Then,' said Mr Tewkesbury, 'you say he took the cigarette out of the packet very slowly?'

'I do,' I said.

'Are you able to say that the slowness was not due to the fact that one cigarette was stuck to another?'

'I can't say that for certain.'

'Well then,' Mr Tewkesbury went on, 'you say he took some time to clamber into his lorry. Are you able to say for certain that he didn't suffer from arthritis or rheumatism, or something of that kind?'

'He walked ordinarily enough,' I said.

'The people who suffer from arthritis or rheumatism or like do sometimes walk ordinarily enough, don't they?' asked Mr Tewkesbury.

'That's true,' I agreed.

'I suffer from arthritis,' said Mr Tewkesbury. 'Did you, for example, see me walk to my place in the court this morning?'

'Yes,' I said, 'I noticed you stumbled.'

'That was not due to arthritis, your honour,' said Mr Tewkesbury.

'No,' I said, 'I thought not.'

'In any event, your honour,' said Mr Tewkesbury, 'you can't say that my client didn't suffer from one of the ailments I've mentioned.'

'No,' I admitted, 'I can't.'

'Then,' said Mr Tewkesbury, 'you say he took a long time when seated in his cab before starting off?'

'Yes.'

'D'you know whether his engine was overheated or not?'

'No, I don't.'

'Is it not possible that he was waiting a little for it to cool down before starting?'

'He didn't seem to wait long enough for that,' I said.

'But all this lighting of a cigarette and slowly clambering into the lorry might have been deliberately to take up time to allow the engine to cool. You can't swear that was not the case,' said Mr Tewkesbury.

'I should be surprised if it was,' I said, 'but I can't swear that it wasn't.'

'Then,' went on Mr Tewkesbury, 'you say that, having started the engine, he took some time before moving off?'

'Yes.'

'Are you able to say that the reason why he waited with the engine running was not because he wanted it to warm up a little before starting?'

The deputy-judge intervened.

'Mr Tewkesbury,' he said, 'I thought you said he wanted it to cool down?'

'Your honour,' said Mr Tewkesbury, 'these are hypothetical questions.'

'Very hypothetical, I should say,' said the deputy-judge.

'Finally,' said Mr Tewkesbury, 'you complain that, as he passed you, he asked you if you were in a hurry. Were you in a hurry?'

'Yes.'

'Why do you object to my client asking the question, then?'

'Like everything else,' I said, 'it was the way he did it. He asked it in a sneering way.'

Mr Tewkesbury then concluded his cross-examination. I had a feeling that it might well be true that he did things better when rather pickled than when completely sober.

Then Mr Smith was called into the witness box and took the oath, and Mr Tewkesbury began to examine him.

'Now, Mr Smith,' he said, 'have you a very great respect for every one of Her Majesty's judges?'

'Yus,' said Mr Smith.

'And, if there is one judge above all for whom you have the deepest respect, who is it?'

'Yus,' said Mr Smith.

'I'll rephrase the question,' said Mr Tewkesbury. 'Have you got the greatest possible respect for his honour the judge of the Willesden County Court?'

'Yus,' said Mr Smith.

'A little leading, wasn't it, Mr Tewkesbury?' queried the deputy-judge.

'Oh, your honour, I was only seeking to save your honour's time,' said Mr Tewkesbury. 'I remember that great judge, Mr Justice Hornet, once said to me when he was at the bar, and I was instructing him in an extremely difficult commercial case where the issues were highly complicated and – '

'Mr Tewkesbury,' said the deputy-judge, 'I thought you said you wanted to save time.'

'The rebuke is well merited, your honour,' said Mr Tewkesbury. 'I will get on with the business in hand. Now, Mr Smith, did you in any way intend to insult his honour the judge of this court, who, as you've said, you hold in the greatest possible respect?'

'Yus,' said Mr Smith.

'That is one of the dangers of leading questions, Mr Tewkesbury,' said the deputy-judge.

'Too true, your honour,' said Mr Tewkesbury. 'I'll rephrase *that* question. When you met the judge in the street, Mr Smith, you didn't want to insult him, did you?'

'I didn't want to insult no one,' said Mr Smith.

'Mr Smith,' asked the deputy-judge, 'did you intend to insult the judge?'

'What should I want to do that for?' said Mr Smith.

'Well, as you ask me, Mr Smith,' said the deputy-judge, 'you might have got some pleasure out of it. Some people do get pleasure from insulting other people. Any further questions, Mr Tewkesbury?'

'No thank you, your honour.'

'Now, Mr Smith,' said the deputy-judge, 'kindly pay attention to me and think before you answer my questions. The answers may be very important to you. D'you understand me?'

'Yus.'

'D'you remember his honour telling you that he was judge of this court?'

'Yus.'

'Did you believe him when he said that?'

'Yus.'

'Did you believe him when he told you that there were a lot of people waiting for him, and he didn't want to be late?'

'Yus.'

'Then why didn't you move your lorry to let him through? – Well, why didn't you?'

'I'd still some bags to deliver.'

'I dare say you had, but it wouldn't have hurt you to have moved the lorry a foot before you'd finished delivering them, would it? – Well, would it?'

'Would it what?'

'Would it have hurt you to have stopped delivering the coal, and to have moved your lorry a foot?'

'It needed more than that.'

'How many feet would you have had to move it?'

'Three feet at least.'

'Would it have been any more trouble to move it three feet than one foot?'

'I hadn't finished the delivery.'

'I know you hadn't. But, if you were going to stop delivering to move the lorry, it made no difference whether you moved it one foot or twenty feet.'

'I didn't have to move it twenty feet,' said Mr Smith.

'I know you didn't,' said the deputy-judge. 'But there is no difference between one foot and twenty feet, is there?'

'If I might assist your honour,' said Mr Tewkesbury, 'my secretary here, who is very good at figures, says the difference is nineteen feet, your honour.'

'Be quiet, Mr Tewkesbury,' said the deputy-judge, 'and behave yourself.'

Mr Tewkesbury rose in his most dignified, drunken manner.

'Your honour,' he said, 'I must protest. I have done nothing to merit your honour's castigation. I have been sitting here like the respectable solicitor I am, and, like the helpful solicitor I hope I am, I merely intervened to assist your honour with the matter of figures. If I've insulted your honour by assuming that your honour could not work them out for yourself, I can only say that if your honour couldn't work them out, your honour would be in what I may say with all due humility, very good company – my own.'

'Sit down, Mr Tewkesbury,' said the deputy-judge.

'Under protest,' said Mr Tewkesbury, 'your honour, I subside.'

'Now, Mr Smith,' went on the deputy-judge. 'Once you were in the cab, it made no difference to you how many feet you moved the lorry?'

'Once I was in the cab,' said Mr Smith, 'I drove away.'

'But not before you'd finished delivering the coal?'

'Of course not, that's what I'm paid for.'

'Why did you ask the judge if he was in a hurry?'

'It looked as if he was.'

'Then why ask him?'

'To pass the time of day, like.'

'Mr Smith,' asked the deputy-judge, 'have you ever heard the expression, "take the mickey out of someone"?'

'Yus,' said Mr Smith.

'What does it mean?'

'What you're doing now,' said Mr Smith.

'You think I'm trying to take the mickey out of you?' asked the deputy-judge.

'It stands to reason, don't it?' said Mr Smith.

'Did you try to take the mickey out of the judge?'

'What should I want to do that for? He hadn't done me no harm.'

'He'd been perfectly polite and courteous to you?' asked the deputy-judge.

'Yus.'

'Then why didn't you respond by giving way to him?'

'I did when I'd finished delivering the coal.'

That concluded Mr Smith's evidence. Mr Tewkesbury then addressed the deputy-judge.

'With all the confidence at my command, and I have a great deal of confidence, particularly in this case,' he said, 'I submit that at the lowest the charge has not been proved. You've got to be satisfied beyond all reasonable doubt that my client, a married man of good character with three small children, that such a man intended to insult the judge. How can you be satisfied on this evidence? I submit you can't be.'

'Thank you, Mr Tewkesbury,' said the deputy-judge. 'In this case I've no doubt whatever that Mr Smith insulted the judge, and intended to do so. The more difficult question I have to decide is what penalty to impose. When I've finally considered the matter, I may find it necessary to impose a sentence of imprisonment. But for two reasons I shall not do so today. In the first place I want to think about the matter more, and secondly, if Mr Smith is to go to prison, I'd like him to have the opportunity of making the necessary arrangements at home. Accordingly I shall adjourn this matter until 10.30 in the morning.'

So the case was adjourned, and I went home. I was a little worried at the outcome. Mr Benton was a very able practitioner, and had sat as a deputy-judge before. But I feared the possibility that unconsciously he might be swayed by the fact that I was the judge of a court where he frequently practised. Mr Smith had undoubtedly behaved very badly, but, if every driver who behaved badly were sent to prison just for that, prison building would be a matter of top priority. Motorists are sometimes not very courteous to each other, but it struck me as rather an odd thing that, if the discourteous motorist were discourteous to a prime minister, a leading industrialist or trade unionist, or the Archbishop of Canterbury, prison could not possibly be made the price of the discourtesy. Why should it be different in my case?

I knew that I should be very upset if Mr Smith were sent to prison – not perhaps as upset as he would be – but considerably disturbed. Why should a judge be in a different position from anybody else? Many other people are just as important to the community as judges, and many indeed are far more important.

My car was laid up, and I'd gone home by train. And so I had a good deal of time to think about the matter. As I walked down the road where we lived, my wife came out to meet me. She seemed in a hurry.

'What's up?' I said, when we met.

'Didn't you remember,' she said, 'that you had to meet Uncle George at the Charing Cross Hotel on his way through London? He's just rung up. He's been waiting there half an hour.'

'Oh gracious,' I said, 'I'm terribly sorry, I forgot all about it.'

'You are an oaf, really,' said my wife.

'I think that's mild,' I said. 'What shall I do? Get a taxi?'

'Yes, you'd better,' she said. 'That's why I came to meet you. He's still got another hour to wait, and you can just do it. To use your favourite expression, you are a blithering idiot. Where have you come from anyway? Aren't you rather late?'

'Perhaps a little,' I said, 'but I've come straight from court.'

I caught a taxi, and while I was on my way to Charing Cross, it suddenly occurred to me that, when my wife met me, she knew I was on my way from court. She had called me an oaf and a blithering idiot, and, though her reproaches were well deserved, the words were surely insulting. And here was my wife calling the judge of the Willesden County Court by an insulting name on his way from court. Could I send her to prison for a month, or fine her ten pounds? It would seem very odd if I could. I decided to look up the section of the County Courts Act again, and as a result when I'd looked it up, I asked leave to address deputy-judge Benton the next morning.

'Your honour,' I said, 'I think perhaps I misinterpreted the words of the Act. They say that any person who insults the judge or – and note these words, your honour – any witness or juror going to or coming from the court etc. etc. Surely, your honour, on consideration, this must mean the precincts of the court, and not several hundred yards from it. There's no difference between several hundred yards and several miles. And if, for example, a juror's wife met him on the way home, knowing that he'd been doing jury service, and proceeded to abuse him for some neglect of her, nothing whatever to do with the case, she couldn't possibly be liable to be fined or sent to prison, could she? And if she couldn't, how can Mr Smith be liable now?'

Mr Tewkesbury rose.

'My point exactly, your honour,' he said, 'as I was trying to make clear to your honour yesterday evening.'

And so I'm glad to say the case against Mr Smith was dismissed, and Mr Tewkesbury left the court with his young secretary no doubt very pleased with himself. I can only guess at their conversation. Perhaps it went like this:

'Well, girl,' said Mr Tewkesbury, 'what did you think of that?'

'You were wonderful, Mr Tewkesbury,' said Bella.

'Thank you, girl,' said Mr Tewkesbury. 'I think this calls for a celebration. What would you say to having dinner with me?'

'Oh, Mr Tewkesbury,' said Bella, 'you're a married man, and I'm a good girl.'

'A good girl, eh?' said Mr Tewkesbury. 'Well, never mind, at least you can spell.'

CHAPTER TWO

Free for All

Actions between the proprietors of schools and the
parents of children who have been sent there are
comparatively rare. When they do take place, it is usually
because the parents have withdrawn a child without
giving the necessary notice. There is seldom any good
defence to such claims. Sometimes a child has not been
happy at the school, but it is impossible to say that the
school has broken its contract. Sometimes the parents
have moved their home and want to have the child nearer
to their new home. Sometimes the parents are just short of
money. But in the case of Chilton against Brooke none of
these circumstances applied.

Major-General Brooke sent his son, David, to Mr
Chilton's school. But after two years there he withdrew
him without notice. When Mr Chilton demanded a term's
fees in lieu of notice, the Major-General refused to pay,
and an action was the result. The Major-General's defence
to Mr Chilton's claim was simple, but very unusual. He
complained that the school had turned David into a
professional blackmailer, that this was a plain breach of
contract, and that in consequence he was entitled to
remove David from the school as soon as he learned what
had happened to him.

The school of which Mr Chilton was proprietor was called 'Freedom House', and, as its name suggested, it was run upon comparatively unusual lines. It was perhaps a little surprising that a soldier should have sent his son there. But the Major-General was not a typical soldier. There came a time when he realised that there were other desirable things in life besides discipline. It was essential in the army, and to some extent at home. But, the Major-General thought, there was something to be said for a mixture of discipline and freedom. So, when he read about 'Freedom House', he decided to give it a trial, and David was sent there.

The boy appeared to enjoy himself at school, and certainly during the holidays he was a happy, healthy boy. It was only after two years that the Major-General discovered to his horror that David had become an accomplished little criminal. David's father acted at once, withdrew him from the school, and refused to pay the claim which was subsequently made upon him.

When the case came on before me, both sides were represented by counsel, the plaintiff by Mr Benton, and the Major-General by Mr Boyd. In opening the case Mr Benton informed me that the school was not quite like other schools. He said that the greatest freedom was given to the pupils.

'It is, of course, possible,' he said, 'that the boy in question was under considerable restraint at home, and that, when he went back for the holidays after learning to enjoy his freedom, this development was not appreciated by his parents.'

'If that is so,' went on Mr Benton, 'all I can say is that Major-General Brooke knew perfectly well the sort of school it was. In fact he visited it during the winter before his son went there, and he was severely snowballed on the way out. When he complained to my client, he said that, if the Major-General didn't like it, he knew what he could do about it.'

'D'you mean to say,' I asked, 'that he still sent his boy to the school after that?'

'I do, your honour,' said Mr Benton, 'and I rely very strongly on the fact that not only did he send him to the school after that, but he kept him there for two whole years.'

Mr Benton then called Mr Chilton to give evidence. Mr Chilton was a tall man with a domed head, and he looked and talked rather like Mr Robert Morley. After he had been sworn and given formal evidence about himself and his school, Mr Benton asked him: 'When the Major-General came to see the school before he sent David to it, did he see the boys?'

'He did indeed,' said Mr Chilton.

'Did he see them at work, or play, or both?'

'Both.'

'What form did the play take?' asked Mr Benton.

'We don't differentiate between work and play,' was the reply.

'Well, what form did the work take?'

'The same as the play.'

'What did the Major-General see the boys doing?'

'Playing.'

'What form did the play take?'

'Work.'

'What form did the work take?'

'Playing.'

I could not resist intervening. 'But what did they *do*?' I asked.

'You may well ask,' said Mr Chilton. 'What didn't they do! They did everything. Helter skelter all over the place.'

'But did they learn nothing?' I asked.

'They learned to play.'

'But what about work?'

'The same thing.'

Mr Benton then joined in.

'What about examinations, Mr Chilton?'

'I don't hold with examinations.'

'Did none of your boys ever pass an examination?' I asked.

'Certainly not,' said Mr Chilton, 'he'd have been expelled if he had.'

'I should like to know,' I said, 'what advantage of any kind your pupils got from coming to your school.'

'They got an advantage,' said Mr Chilton, 'which is denied probably to all other boys in all other schools. For the only time in their lives they had complete freedom.'

'Could they do anything they liked?' I asked.

'Yes,' said Mr Chilton.

'Suppose they hit you?' I asked.

'I hit them back harder,' said Mr Chilton. 'We're free as well, you see. It's a wonderful sight, your honour, to see masters and boys all perfectly free to do whatever they want. Perhaps you'd like to come and see for yourself one day?'

'Not, I think, when there is snow on the ground, thank you,' I said.

Mr Benton brought the witness to the incident of the snowball.

'There's nothing to it,' said Mr Chilton. 'One of the boys had put a stone in a snowball so that it hurt the Major-General when it hit him. But he was free to go, as I explained.'

'Are you telling me, Mr Chilton,' I asked, 'that the Major-General realised that, if their boy came to your school, he would learn nothing at all?'

'Certainly not, your honour,' said Mr Chilton. 'He would learn a great deal. He did learn a great deal. I think I can say he was the most accomplished blackmailer we've ever turned out.'

'That is exactly what the defendant complains about,' I said.

'There's no justification whatever for the complaint,' said Mr Chilton.

'I don't understand,' I said. 'I thought you said that the boy became an accomplished blackmailer.'

'Certainly.'

'But that's what the Major-General complains about.'

'I repeat,' said Mr Chilton, 'that there is no justification for his complaint. If he left my school as a blackmailer, he came as one. The great advantage of coming to my school is this. My methods bring out the best and worst in a boy. By free association together the boys learn all sorts of things which they have no chance of learning anywhere else. The things they learn may be good or bad. That is human nature. There is much good and bad in all of us. But my theory is that, if a boy's got a lot of bad in him and is likely to become, say, a blackmailer in later life, it's very much better for it to be brought out straightaway. Then it can be corrected. On the other hand, if you keep it under and the boy, on the face of it, behaves himself, the repressed desire to blackmail may come out at a much later stage, and the boy may become an ugly criminal when it is too late to do anything about it except to send him to prison for many years.'

'So you don't actually teach blackmail?' I inquired.

24

'There are no lectures on the subject,' said Mr Chilton. 'There are no lectures on any subject.'

'But the boys are free to blackmail, or burgle, or however the fancy takes them?'

'Of course, within the grounds of the school. I don't let them pillage the local houses or shops or I might get into trouble myself.'

'So a lot of stealing goes on?' I asked.

'Certainly. Other schools may turn out university scholars and international rugger players, but what's the good of all that if they subsequently get three years for false pretences? I can tell your honour that some of my worst boys are now pillars of the Church.'

'But what about the good ones?' I asked. 'What do they learn?'

'They learn life, your honour,' said Mr Chilton. 'This is a subject of which most educational authorities, most lawyers, and most other professional men seem strikingly ignorant. What is the good of a knowledge of classics and mathematics if you don't know how to live with your fellow men? An ounce of freedom is worth a pound of Liddell and Scott and Lewis and Short put together.'

'How long have you been carrying on this school, Mr Chilton?' I asked.

'For fifteen years.'

'Successfully?'

'Very successfully. With one qualification.'

'And what,' I asked, 'is the qualification?'

'The Inland Revenue, your honour.'

In due course Mr Chilton was cross-examined by counsel for the Major-General.

'Mr Chilton,' he asked as his first question, 'during your fifteen years you must have had at least one or two boys who were by nature very bad indeed.'

'More than that, sir,' said Mr Chilton.

'Some of them,' went on counsel, 'so bad that they would be prepared to commit murder?'

'And worse, sir,' said Mr Chilton.

'How many murders,' asked counsel, 'have you totted up during your regime?'

'Actual murders?' replied Mr Chilton. 'None, sir. But we've had some very fine attempts.'

'So,' said counsel, 'you have a boy sent to your school, and you send him back home to his parents as a murderer.'

'If we send him home as a murderer,' said Mr Chilton, 'he came as one.'

'Then,' said counsel, 'he may murder his parents.'

'That is quite possible,' said Mr Chilton. 'But if so, he'd have probably murdered them anyway. Such a boy's parents stand a much better chance of keeping their lives by having their son's murderous instincts brought out early. I expect we've saved a good many lives this way. And the same applies to David. Blackmail is moral murder. If we'd bottled up the blackmail in him, it might have come out as actual murder. I can assure you that David Brooke was a very nasty little boy when he came to us, and an even nastier one when he left us.'

'What good does that do to his parents?' asked counsel.

'A great deal of good, sir,' said Mr Chilton. 'We send a complete report on each boy at the end of each term. We told your client exactly all we knew about David, so that for the first time the parents learned what a horrible little reptile they'd been nurturing. Knowing that, they can take remedial measures.'

'Why don't *you* take remedial measures?' I asked.

'That's normally quite impossible,' said Mr Chilton.

I asked why.

'Usually, the boy isn't with us long enough. You see, your honour, it's no small thing to bring out the worst in a boy. And it may take a very long time. Sometimes when we think we've got to the dregs, we find there is something even worse below. Life is short, your honour. The part of it that you spend at school is even shorter. There is positively no time to carry out both processes. What we do is to discover the best and worst in our boys, and we leave it to the parents to make the most of the results. And it's just as well to know their virtues too, your honour. For example, a few boys have a passion for the truth. Well, it would be no good sending them into politics or law.'

'What should I do with a blackmailer or thief?' I asked.

'Well,' said Mr Chilton, 'I don't know what you'd do with him, your honour. Some parents are blackmailers or thieves themselves, in which case the boy can carry on the family business. But, if it were a boy of mine, I should take remedial measures. What those measures would be would depend entirely upon the individuality of the boy himself. That's another reason why it's quite impossible to carry out such treatment at school. Each boy needs individual treatment, and the best people to provide that treatment are the boy's parents. When they know exactly what is wrong. Major-General Brooke ought to be very grateful to me. David is a very capable young man. If he'd gone to an ordinary school, he'd have very likely gone on to a university and ended in gaol or worse.'

'Worse?' queried counsel.

'Well, for some people, for me for example, just managing to keep out of gaol would be worse than actually going to gaol. I mean never knowing if and when the blow will fail. A boy of David's character would almost certainly have taken to crime at some stage in his career. He might have done very well indeed, up to a point, and then suddenly been completely ruined. Now you can't change his nature, but you can provide against the ill effects of that nature.'

'What do you suggest that David's parents should do?' asked counsel.

'Well,' said Mr Chilton, 'if they were sensible people, what they would do would be this. First of all they'd pay my bill and put an end to these ridiculous proceedings. Then they would talk to David about his future career. With luck, they'd be able to point out one method by which he could give full play, or almost full play, to his great ability in certain respects without offending against the law. He obviously likes extracting money from people by threats. Well, the legal profession is an obvious possibility for him. I'm not quite sure if he likes hurting people, but if he does, he might either become a dentist, or go into the Inland Revenue. The object of life is, in my view, to get as much happiness for oneself while giving as little unhappiness as possible to other people. Schools and universities don't bother about teaching that sort of thing. As I indicated before, nuclear physics and classics and mathematics will not help you to get on with your neighbour.'

'Mr Chilton,' I said, 'one thing has occurred to me. How do you manage to satisfy the local inspector of schools?'

'He daren't come near the place,' said Mr Chilton. 'His predecessor came in a Mini Minor and left in an ambulance. We do it all now by correspondence.'

'As to that,' said counsel, 'my client, Major-General Brooke, might himself have left in an ambulance.'

'Certainly,' said Mr Chilton. 'We had one standing by.'

'Do all your parents have to undergo this ordeal?' asked counsel.

'Not if they don't want to. They can do it all by correspondence too. But I admit they don't learn as much that way. If you really want to know what happens, you've got to come and see for yourself.'

'And,' I put in, 'feel for yourself too, I gather.'

'Oh, certainly,' said Mr Chilton, 'that can happen.'

'Was Major-General Brooke particularly unlucky?' asked counsel.

'Not at all, your honour,' said Mr Chilton. 'On the contrary, I'd say he was one of the lucky ones. He left under his own steam.'

'Have you never been sued for assault or something of that kind?' I asked.

'Certainly not, your honour. All our prospective parents sign a form of indemnity before they come on the premises.'

'Have you any records of the subsequent careers of many of your boys?' asked counsel.

'Yes, sir, we have.'

'And generally speaking, what is their record?'

'Much the same as that for any other good school, with one exception.'

'And what might that be?' asked counsel.

'The crime rate is much lower.'

Eventually Mr Chilton completed his evidence, and the Major-General went into the witness box. In one of counsel's early questions, he was asked whether he was warned what might happen to him when he went down to inspect the school.'

'Well,' said the Major-General, 'Mr Chilton did say that the boys were very boisterous, and that I might be ragged a bit. Well, your honour, I like high spirits and I think I can say I can hold my own in most company. As a matter of fact in my younger days I boxed for the Army, and I thought it would be an interesting experience.'

'Were you hit on the head by a snowball?' asked counsel.

'I was hit on the head by a stone in the guise of a snowball', was the reply.

'Did you complain?' I asked.

'No, your honour. I didn't like the boys to think that I minded, so I treated it as a good joke. I had to put up with a good deal more in the war.'

'But then,' I said, 'you were fighting the Germans.'

'It didn't seem all that different, your honour,' replied the Major-General.

'Why have you refused to pay Mr Chilton's bill, and withdrawn your boy from the school without notice?' he was asked by counsel.

'Because of the way they sent him home. He was physically, morally and mentally degenerate.'

The Major-General was then cross-examined.

'What exactly do you say was wrong with your son when he came home to you?'

'His hair was over his shoulders,' said the Major-General, 'he didn't wash, and he couldn't speak a civil word to us, he stole some of my money and he pawned a silver cup.'

'Which, no doubt,' said counsel, 'you won for boxing?'

'Quite so,' said the Major-General. 'I minded that more than I did the money.'

'Is that the sum total of your complaint?'

'Certainly not. He threatened both his mother and me. He said that he'd leave home if we didn't make him a bigger allowance.'

'General,' said counsel, 'when you sent your boy to the school, you knew it was a pretty odd school?'

'I knew it was different.'

'If the boys were allowed with impunity to throw stones at the parents of prospective pupils, did it not occur to you that there might be other things that they would do which might be even worse?'

'I admit I thought it was roughing it up a bit to put a stone in a snowball, and not altogether sporting. But there was nothing dishonest about it.'

'Wasn't there?' I asked. 'You said yourself that it was a stone in the guise of a snowball. You mightn't particularly mind being hit by a snowball, but if you knew there was a stone in it, you would certainly duck.'

'I did,' said the Major-General.

'But it hit you just the same?'

'Yes.'

'But wouldn't you describe it as dirty play?' asked counsel.

'Yes,' said the Major-General, 'that's exactly how I would describe it. Where games are played, there is always a certain amount of dirty play, and one's got to accept it. But that's very different from plain theft.'

'General,' went on counsel, 'you've heard Mr Chilton say what the theory is behind his method of carrying on the school.'

'Method of carrying on the school!' repeated the Major-General, with scorn. 'It's all a lot of bunkum, sir. If you ask me, the whole thing's a fraud. They get a lot of money from a lot of unsuspecting parents. They do no work at all, and allow the boys to become little hooligans and then that unctuous peacock goes into the witness box and lays down the law as though he were the second Messiah.'

'But, Major-General,' went on counsel, 'you heard Mr Chilton explain that, if the parents of a boy know his criminal tendencies early enough, they may be able to set him on the right road. Whereas if they don't know of them, he may become a criminal when it's too late to do anything for him.'

'I heard your client talk a lot of poppycock,' said the Major-General. 'I didn't ask Mr Chilton to teach my boy Latin or Greek or nuclear physics or mathematics or any of the rest of them. I liked the idea of this lack of restraint. I thought it might be good for a boy in the first instance. I thought it might be character-building. But I expected the end product to be a decent boy who could live in a decent family where you didn't have to lock up the spoons before going to bed.'

'How do you know,' asked counsel, 'that you wouldn't have had to lock up the spoons if he hadn't gone to this school?'

'Well, I've never had to lock them up before.'

'Did you count them all?'

'Of course not.'

'Then how do you know you didn't lose any?'

'Well, I know, that's all. You can tell when things start to become missing. I saw the cup wasn't there on the day when he took it.'

'Well, of course you noticed that,' said counsel, 'as you enjoyed looking at it. Every morning you probably revived old memories.'

'That's perfectly true. Anything wrong in that?' asked the Major-General.

'Of course not,' said counsel, 'but that's why you'd noticed its absence. But the spoons – '

The Major-General interrupted: 'I won some spoons too,' he said.

'Well, you didn't win any forks, did you?' said counsel.

'I can't say that I did.'

'Then,' said counsel, 'unless you counted the forks each day, you couldn't tell if any were missing.'

'My wife would have known,' said the Major-General.

'Well,' said counsel, 'let's assume that he never stole anything from you until he'd been at the plaintiff's school for the six terms you allowed him to be there. When did he first start to steal anything?'

'As far as I know, only during last holidays.'

'So apparently,' I said, 'it took him two years to learn to steal.'

'I suppose so,' said the Major-General.

'Are you complaining that he didn't learn any quicker?' asked counsel.

'I'm complaining that he learned at all.'

'But you can't say that he wasn't a thief by nature ever since he became of an age to think for himself?' asked counsel.

'I can only say,' said the Major-General, 'that until these last holidays, we always found him a decent boy. Of course he wasn't perfect, nobody wanted him to be. But he wasn't a boy any father need be ashamed of.'

'If what Mr Chilton says is right,' I said, 'it won't be necessary for you to be ashamed of him now.'

'If what Mr Chilton said is right, your honour,' said the Major-General, 'we should all be put in lunatic asylums and the inmates should be let out to play about with Mr Chilton and his boys. And run the country too, I suppose,' he added.

'Well,' I said, 'some people think that they are doing that already.'

By that time it was 4.15 and I said that I would adjourn the case until the following morning for the speeches of counsel, and for my judgment.

'But perhaps it may help you,' I added, 'if I tell you what I am thinking provisionally at the moment. The General let his son go to this pretty odd school willingly enough in the first instance, and allowed him to stay there six whole terms. He now says that he doesn't like the results. It's true that the way in which this school is carried on is, to say the least, unusual. But, as far as I can see, the General took a risk of that. Whether or not the method is a good one, whether or not Mr Chilton is right in the views which he has expressed, I think it may be very difficult for a man in the position of the defendant, Major-General Brooke, two years after he sent his son to the school, to say that he's not satisfied with the result, and to refuse to give the proper notice. However, as I said, I will hear the argument in full in the morning.'

In those words I gave a pretty clear indication to counsel that I was in all probability going to decide in favour of Mr Chilton. And it therefore came as a very considerable surprise to me when the next morning arrived, the case was called on and counsel for Mr Chilton got up and said: 'I'm happy to tell your honour that you will no longer be troubled with this case. The parties have come to terms.'

Those terms were that the action was withdrawn and Mr Chilton agreed to pay the whole of the Major-General's costs. I was very much surprised. Both counsel were experienced and able men, and they must have told their clients that the strong probability was that Mr Chilton was going to win. Why then did he completely throw in his hand? Why did he start the action if he was going to do that in the end? I simply did not understand it. But what I did not know then and only learned afterwards was what happened after the court had adjourned.

David Brooke, who had taken no part in the proceedings, had nevertheless been in court the whole time. And, as Mr Chilton was walking home, he came up to him.

'Hello, you scallywag,' said Mr Chilton.

'Hello, sir,' said David. 'Nice to see you.'

'Nice to see you, David,' said Mr Chilton.

'I'm afraid,' said David, 'you may not feel so friendlily disposed towards me in a few minutes.'

'Well, if you want the truth,' said Mr Chilton, 'I've never felt friendlily disposed towards you. I took you on for money, and had to make the best of it. I've done my duty, and now your father's got to do his and pay me.'

'I think not, Mr Chilton,' said David.

'Were you in court, David?'

'The whole time.'

'Well, I don't suppose you're used to courts, or understand what judges say,' said Mr Chilton, 'but I can assure you that the judge indicated in what he said before he left the court that he was going to come down fairly and squarely on my side and make your father pay.'

'I understood that perfectly, Mr Chilton,' said David. 'That's why I'm here. Because my father isn't going to pay.'

'Well, that's a matter for your father,' said Mr Chilton. 'If he's stupid about it, of course the bailiffs will be put in, and I don't know what else. But that's entirely a matter for him. Once I've got a judgment against him, I wash my hands of the affair, the law will take its course.'

'But you aren't going to get a judgment against him, Mr Chilton,' said David.

'You don't even know what a judgment is, David,' said Mr Chilton.

'Oh yes, indeed I do, and you aren't going to ask for a judgment against my father.'

'Well, my counsel will.'

'No, your counsel won't, Mr Chilton.'

'Well, you come there in the morning and see.'

'I shall come there in the morning, Mr Chilton, but I shan't see. At least I shan't see what you said I shall see.'

'Well,' said Mr Chilton, 'there's no point in arguing with you.'

'I quite agree,' said David, 'no point at all. But I just want to tell you something. As you rightly said in court, I learned a good number of things at your school, breaking and entering as well as blackmail.'

'Which did you prefer?' asked Mr Chilton.

'On the whole,' said David, 'blackmail. Though breaking and entering can help. For example, Mr Chilton,' went on David, 'I broke into your study, and bearing in mind that, if a thing is worth doing, it's worth doing well, I broke open your safe.'

'I didn't find anything missing,' said Mr Chilton.

'I didn't take anything,' said David.

'Good.'

'Except – ' said David.

'Except what?' asked Mr Chilton.

'Except information,' said David.

'I hope you profit by it, David,' said Mr Chilton.

'That is what I'm about to do,' said David. 'Mr Chilton, you mentioned during your evidence that you didn't like the Inland Revenue. Well, that's no crime. Lots of people don't like the Inland Revenue. But to keep two different sets of books, one for the Inland Revenue, and one to enable you to count your gains when the shop is closed, I believe is not only contrary to moral principles, but also to the law of the land. And unless, Mr Chilton, you can persuade me not to do so, I'm going to convey to the Inspector of Inland Revenue the information I obtained in the way that I've just told you.'

'Blackmail, David,' said Mr Chilton.

'Well, you shouldn't be surprised,' said David. 'You seem to be rather proud of me.'

'Now, David,' said Mr Chilton, 'that's all very well. Blackmail is one of the most serious crimes known to the law.'

'I've been looking it up,' said David, 'I agree.'

'Well,' said Mr Chilton, 'if I go to a policeman and tell him what you've been doing, not only will you be charged with blackmail, but they won't give me away because otherwise no one would ever go to the police when they are being blackmailed. Really, David, I'm rather grateful to you. I *have* sometimes rather worried about my double set of books. What I said in the witness box about fear of prison in some ways being worse than prison itself was quite true, but you've given me the answer, David. We shall now go to the police station where I shall confess my own fault, and accuse you of yours. Mine will be forgiven me, and you will go to prison or a detention centre or some place of safe custody for many, many years. I'm sorry that it should have to be through me, David, but perhaps after all there is some poetic justice in that. You can think of that when you are pacing up and down your cell.'

'If either of us is going to be pacing up and down his cell,' said David, 'it won't be me, Mr Chilton, but you. Let us go to a police station by all means, and let me tell you what will happen. You will confess that you've been keeping a double set of books and accuse me of blackmail. The sergeant will look up the law. He will then ask you what actually is the offence with which you charge Mr David Brooke. And you will say, "threatening to accuse me of a crime if I don't withdraw the proceedings against his father," and the sergeant will say: "What crime is that, Mr Chilton?" And you will put your hand through what hair you have left and probably say: "Well, it must be blackmail." Well, don't take it from me, Mr Chilton, but I can assure you it isn't. You go to your solicitors, or you go to the police and they will tell you. I'm asking for nothing for myself. My father hasn't the faintest idea that I'm doing this. He'd be horrified if he knew. Now, Mr Chilton, would you like to go to that police station and confess that you keep two sets of books? Or will you instruct your counsel in the morning to give up your claim?'

Mr Chilton did not say anything for a moment, and then: 'When I said that you were the nastiest little boy I'd ever seen,' he said, 'it was an understatement. Now go to hell. You know the way, I see.'

I was told that later that evening David approached his father.

'I'm sorry the case is going against you, father,' he said, 'what'll it cost?'

'I don't so much mind the money, David,' said his father, 'but it's losing to that self-satisfied, mealy-mouthed scoundrel of a schoolmaster that troubles me. I hate the thought of it.'

'Would you like to win the case, father?' asked David.

'Of course I would. I'd give a good deal to win it.'

'How much? £50?'

'More.'

'I'll settle for £50,' said David.

'What d'you mean?' said his father.

'If you win the case,' said David, 'will you give me £50.'

'All right,' said his father, 'I will. I'd much rather give you £50 for nothing than pay a penny to that so-and-so.'

'Done, father,' said David, 'Can I have it in fivers?'

'I only hope you get it.'

'I'll get it all right, father. You have it ready to give me as soon as the judge gives judgment for you.'

And, when next day came round, to the Major-General's surprise, as well as to mine, Mr Chilton withdrew the case and agreed to pay the defendant's costs.

'I've never been so pleased to pay out on a wager, my boy,' said his father as he gave the £50 to David. 'And you got it by fair means this time, no false pretences, no blackmail, nothing. All fair and above board, you've earned it.'

'Yes, I think I've earned it, father,' said David.

'And now, my boy,' said his father, 'have you had any more thought about what you're going to do?'

'I think,' said David, 'I'd like to follow in grandfather's footsteps.'

'But he was a bishop,' said his father.

'That's right,' said David.

I remembered then that Mr Chilton had said that some of his worst boys had become pillars of the Church.

CHAPTER THREE

Perjury

The offence of perjury strikes at the root of justice. But, in my opinion, many lawyers and laymen do not treat it seriously enough. A man charged with a crime is pretty well given a free licence to commit as much perjury as he likes in his attempts to be acquitted of the crime with which he's charged. The amount of perjury committed in criminal trials is tremendous. Every day men and women are swearing what they know to be false. But prosecutions after a conviction or an acquittal of a man who has committed perjury in the witness box are extremely rare. I do not pretend that the problem in the case of criminal trials is an easy one. Up to seventy years ago an accused person was not allowed to give evidence at all. That is obviously highly unsatisfactory. But now we seem to have gone to the other extreme. The reason why prisoners were not allowed to give evidence before 1898 was ecclesiastical in origin. It was feared that they might perjure their immortal souls in their efforts to escape conviction. It is not easy to find the solution which will at the same time give prisoners the right to give evidence on oath, and nevertheless make them less inclined to break that oath.

But, while the solution in criminal trials is admittedly very difficult to find, that is no reason at all why in civil cases, where no man's liberty is involved, the danger of a man being charged with perjury should not be much greater. I have had a number of cases where one side or the other was committing plain and provable perjury, but no proceedings for perjury were taken.

The present story is a good example of a case where one side swore black, and the other side swore white, and the answer was not grey. In other words, deliberate perjury was being committed, but by whom? That was the question.

The story started with a dispute between two motorists. I will call them Morris and Riley. They nearly had a collision and this was entirely due to the fault of Morris. Mr Riley was very angry and ran up to Morris' car, and, in spite of the apologies which Morris tendered profusely, proceeded to assault him. In consequence, Mr Morris sued Mr Riley for assault. And in those proceedings he not only claimed damages for the injuries to himself, but for breaking a gold watch. He said that when he put up his hands to prevent Mr Riley's blows landing on his face, they struck the watch and broke it.

After the case had been opened by counsel, Mr Morris gave his evidence and told me what had happened. Apart from one matter, his story was not seriously disputed by the defendant. But it was that one matter which made the case of more than usual interest.

After Mr Morris had been cross-examined for a few minutes by Mr Faulkner, counsel for Mr Riley, he was asked this question: 'Now, Mr Morris, you're claiming the cost of a new watch from my client, aren't you?'

'Not the cost of a new one,' said Mr Morris, 'the value of the old.'

'If you please,' said Mr Faulkner, 'the value of the old. And you say that the watch which you produced ten minutes ago is the watch which my client damaged?'

'Certainly.'

'Will you look at it, please,' said Mr Faulkner. 'Hand it to him please, usher.'

The usher duly took it to the witness, who looked at it.

'Yes,' said Mr Morris, 'I have it in front of me.'

'Look at it, please,' said Mr Faulkner.

'I am looking at it.'

'Do you say on oath,' said Mr Faulkner, 'that that is your watch?'

'I've already said it on oath.'

'I want to be sure,' said Mr Faulkner, 'that there's no mistake. Is that the watch which Mr Riley damaged when he struck you?'

At that stage I intervened to ask: 'Mr Faulkner, your client then admits the assault?'

'Certainly, your honour,' said Mr Faulkner, 'but not the damage.'

'You mean,' I asked, 'that you say that this is not the watch which was damaged?'

'Precisely,' said Mr Faulkner.

'It is his face, I suppose?' I asked.

'Oh yes,' said Mr Faulkner, 'I admit the face, and that my client struck it. I also admit that my client would have struck it a second time, but Mr Morris' hand got in the way.'

'Was there a watch on it?' I asked.

'My client has no idea,' said Mr Faulkner. 'All we say is that, whether or not the plaintiff had a watch, it is not this one.'

'Very strange,' I said, 'if it isn't.'

'Stranger things have happened in this court,' said Mr Faulkner, who, it will be gathered, was not an advocate who was frightened to express himself.

'Give me an example,' I suggested.

'Oh, your honour,' said Mr Faulkner, 'I hadn't any particular event in mind. But very strange things do happen in the courts from time to time. Let me think. Yes, your honour. I once cross-examined a witness who turned out to have exactly the same name and address as I had.'

'As you had?' I asked.

'Yes, your honour. As I had. He was Jeremy Faulkner, and he lived at eighteen Greenfield Gardens, and so do I.'

'It wasn't you, I suppose?' I asked.

'The towns were different, your honour, but it was a very odd coincidence.'

'And what precisely has this got to do with the case?' I asked.

'Your honour, you asked for an example of something strange. It was the first I could think of.'

'Quite right, Mr Faulkner,' I said. 'I apologise. Now let's get on. Mr Morris, d'you say you had a wristwatch on when you were assaulted?'

'I do, your honour.'

'And that this was the watch?'

'Yes, your honour.'

'No doubt about it?'

'None at all, your honour.'

'Very well then, pray continue, Mr Faulkner.'

'I suggest to you, Mr Morris,' went on Mr Faulkner, 'that you are deliberately telling a lie.'

'Can you tell a lie by mistake, Mr Faulkner?' I asked. 'You can tell an untruth by accident, but a lie is surely a deliberate untruth, isn't it?'

43

'I plead guilty to a pleonasm,' said Mr Faulkner. 'Now, Mr Morris, when you say that this is the watch which was damaged by my client, you're telling a lie, aren't you?'

'Certainly not.'

'I suggest to you, Mr Morris, that you acquired this watch three days ago, from the landlord of the Barclay Arms, Trenton.'

'Nonsense,' said Mr Morris.

'Let Mr Carr stand up, please,' said Mr Faulkner, and a man stood up in the back of the court. 'D'you see that gentleman?' went on Mr Faulkner.

'I do.'

'Have you seen him before?'

'I have.'

'He's the landlord of the Barclay Arms, isn't he?'

'I know. I often have a drink there.'

At that stage, Mr Carr spoke up from the back of the court:

'Look,' he shouted, 'I don't want to get involved in this. I – '

But the usher broke in with: 'Silence in court!'

'Mr Faulkner,' I asked, 'are you calling that gentleman as a witness?'

'I am, your honour.'

'Well, would you please tell him to keep quiet until his turn comes.'

'I don't want my turn to come,' shouted Mr Carr.

'Silence in court,' said the usher.

'Keep quiet, sir,' I said.

'Why should I be mixed up in their affairs?' shouted Mr Carr.

I asked Mr Carr to come forward, and he did so.

'Now, Mr Carr, you are the landlord of the Barclay Arms?'

'Yes, sir,' he said, 'I am, and I want to get back there.'

'I dare say you do, Mr Carr,' I said, 'but, if you're a witness, I'm afraid you'll have to remain.'

'It isn't fair,' said Mr Carr. 'There's a lot to do to get ready for opening, and I've only got a young boy who knows nothing about it to help me.'

'I'm extremely sorry,' I said.

'Some people think pubs run themselves,' went on Mr Carr. 'Well, they don't. There's a hell of a lot of work to do, or we'd go bust in no time.'

'You're not in your public house now, Mr Carr,' I said, 'and you're not to talk like that. I know it's inconvenient for people sometimes, but the courts couldn't be carried on unless witnesses could be compelled to attend.'

'I quite understand that, your honour,' said Mr Carr, 'in a case of importance. Murder or something. But this petty squabble shouldn't involve other people. If they were sensible, it could be settled over a pint.'

'That could well be, Mr Carr,' I said, 'but I'm afraid I can't discuss the matter any more. Kindly sit down and keep quiet.'

So the disgruntled Mr Carr went back to his seat in the court, and Mr Faulkner continued to question Mr Morris.

'Mr Morris,' he asked, 'did you not buy this watch from Mr Carr for £4 three nights ago?'

'Nonsense, why should I?'

'You're not supposed to ask me questions,' said Mr Faulkner, 'but I don't mind answering that one. If my client didn't damage any watch of yours, you might want to increase the damages by pretending that he did. I suggest that's what you've done.'

'If I never speak another word,' said Mr Morris loudly, 'I tell you that he broke my watch when he lashed out at me. It's absolutely true, your honour.'

He said it very convincingly. I said as much, and added: 'I take it you want to pursue this point, Mr Faulkner, and to continue to keep Mr Carr from his public house?'

'I'm afraid so, your honour,' said Mr Faulkner.

'Now, Mr Morris,' he went on, 'will you kindly look at someone else. Will Mr Briggs stand up, please. D'you know him by sight?'

'I don't think so.'

'He also goes to the Barclay Arms.'

'I don't know everyone who goes there.'

'I don't suggest you do, but he remembers you.'

'What am I supposed to say to that?'

'He's going to say that he provided the watch which the landlord sold to you, and that this is the watch.'

'I'm on oath,' said Mr Morris.

'I know you are,' said Mr Faulkner, 'and so will he be. Do you still deny it?'

'Of course I do. It's all a put-up job to get out of paying for what was quite a valuable watch.'

Eventually Mr Morris' cross-examination was concluded, and in due course Mr Carr and Mr Briggs gave evidence. Mr Carr did so most unwillingly, but, if ever there was a voluntary witness, it was Mr Briggs. He obviously enjoyed himself from beginning to end.

'You are Edward Briggs,' said Mr Faulkner, 'and you live at seven, Maryland Buildings, E6?'

'Yes.'

'What are you, Mr Briggs?'

'Yes.'

'What d'you mean by "yes"?'

'I was told I had to say "yes" or "no", and "yes" sounded more like.'

'Well,' I put in, 'you don't have just to say "yes" or "no", Mr Briggs, answer the questions as you like.'

'Oh, that's different,' said Mr Briggs.

'So long as you tell the truth,' I added.

'The truth, eh, my lord? That's asking a bit.'

'I know,' I said, 'but you must do your best.'

'OK my lord, what's the question?

'What do you do for a living?' asked Mr Faulkner.

'Sell fings.'

'Such as?'

'That's right.'

'What d'you sell?'

'What do I sell? Logs and dogs.'

'I beg your pardon.'

'Granted.'

'*What do you sell?*'

'Told yer. Logs and dogs.'

'Logs and dogs?'

'Logs *and* dogs.'

'That's an odd combination,' said Mr Faulkner.

'What's that?' said Mr Briggs.

'Logs and dogs.'

'Logs and dogs,' repeated Mr Briggs.

'What's wrong with selling logs and dogs, Mr Faulkner?' I asked.

'Oh nothing, your honour,' he said, 'except they don't seem to go together.'

'Look,' said Mr Briggs. 'I sell logs, see. And sometimes I pick up a dog or two cheap, see. So I sell 'em. That's logs and dogs, ain't it?'

'Oh, yes,' said Mr Faulkner, 'it's logs and dogs.'

'Well that's me then,' said Mr Briggs. 'Logs and dogs.'

'Have you seen Mr Morris before?' asked Mr Faulkner.

'Yes.'

'Where?'

'In the boozer.'

'You mean the Barclay Arms?' I put in.

'Yes.'

'When did you last see him before today?' asked Mr Faulkner.

'In the boozer?'

'All right, Mr Briggs,' I said, 'in the boozer.'

'Didn't see you there, my lord,' said Mr Briggs.

'No, you wouldn't have,' I said.

'Perhaps it's the wig?'

'No,' I said, 'it's not the wig.'

'There's nothing wrong in going to a boozer, is there?' said Mr Briggs.

'Nothing at all,' I said.

'Then why don't you go, my lord?' asked Mr Briggs.

'Mr Faulkner,' I said, 'shall we get on with the case?'

'Mr Briggs,' said Mr Faulkner, 'when did you last see Mr Morris in the Barclay Arms?'

'A couple of nights ago,' said Mr Briggs. 'Call me a liar, it was three, or I'm a Dutchman. Cor, I am a Dutchman, it was four.'

'Well, whenever it was,' said Mr Faulkner, 'what happened?'

'Well,' said Mr Briggs, 'I was downing my pint quiet like, when I heard him say something funny to Mr Carr.'

'What did he say?'

'He said he wanted to buy a gold watch.'

'What was funny about that?'

'He said he wanted one that didn't go,' said Mr Briggs.

'He wanted to buy a gold watch that didn't go?' I asked.

'That's right, my lord.'

'So what did you do?' asked Mr Faulkner.

'I listened,' said Mr Briggs. 'I thought I might do a bit of business.'

'Why?' I asked, 'Had you a gold watch that didn't go?'

'Oh, no, my lord,' said Mr Briggs. 'I've nothing gold about me. But I thought I might pick one up.'

'How,' I asked, 'pick one up? Among the logs and dogs?'

'That's right, my lord.'

'You mean,' I asked, 'that you thought you might find a watch among the logs and dogs?'

'In a manner of speaking, yes, my lord.'

'Explain, please,' I said.

'Well, my lord,' said Mr Briggs, 'it's like this. I sell logs and dogs. Now 'ow can I do that if I don't buy them? I can't, see. So I *buy* logs and dogs.'

'We all know that by now,' I said, 'but where does the watch come in?'

'Well,' said Mr Briggs, 'blokes what sell dogs may sell other things too.'

'Such as?' said Mr Faulkner.

'Yes,' said Mr Briggs.

'What other things?' said Mr Faulkner.

'All sorts. Stands to reason. If you can pick up a dog, you can pick up a lot of other things.'

'Such as a watch?' I asked.

'You've got it, my lord,' said Mr Briggs.

'So what did you do?' asked Mr Faulkner.

'After this bloke had gone, I told Mr Carr I might be able to oblige him.'

'And then?'

'I went to the club. There's all sorts there.'

'And what happened when you went to the club?'

'I found a man with a gold watch, and I bought it for two nicker. Then I sold it to Mr Carr for three.'

'Thank you,' said Mr Faulkner, and sat down.

Mr Briggs was then cross-examined by Mr Morris' counsel, whose name was Meldrum.

'Mr Briggs, have you told his honour the truth?' was his first question.

'Near enough.'

'How d'you mean, near enough?'

'What I say, near enough.'

'Most of what you say has been lies, hasn't it?'

'Me tell lies?'

'That's right.'

'Wouldn't do such a thing.'

'Have you never told a lie?'

'Only to the missus,' said Mr Briggs. 'But we all do that, don't we, my lord?'

'Go on, please, Mr Meldrum,' I said.

'I suggest that your story is a lie from beginning to end,' said Mr Meldrum. 'You never heard my client ask to buy a watch which didn't go. You never bought a watch in your club. You never sold it to Mr Carr. And Mr Carr never sold it to Mr Morris.'

'I never said he did,' said Mr Briggs.

'I thought the whole case was,' said Mr Meldrum, 'that Mr Carr sold this watch to Mr Morris.'

'So it is,' said Mr Faulkner, 'but Mr Briggs didn't see that part of the transaction.'

'I see,' said Mr Meldrum. 'Very well then, Mr Briggs, you only heard Mr Morris ask to buy it. You never saw him get it from Mr Carr?'

'That's right.'

'But, when you heard the conversation in which Mr Morris said he wanted a watch which didn't go, you thought there might have been a bit of business in it for you?'

'That's right.'

'So off you go to the club, and lo and behold! there's a man with a gold watch ready to sell it to you for two pounds.'

'That's right.'

'Was it by chance a watch which didn't go?'

'Not when I bought it,' said Mr Briggs, 'but I put that right before I sold it to Mr Carr.'

'A bit of luck for you that on the very day you want a watch, you find one,' said Mr Meldrum.

'That's life,' said Mr Briggs.

'What was the name of the man who sold you the watch?'

'Can't remember.'

'Did you ever know it?'

'Can't say that I did.'

'Had you ever seen him before?'

'Can't say that I had?'

'Have you ever seen him since?'

'Can't say that I have.'

'Would you recognise him again?'

'I might. And then again I might not.'

'You wouldn't happen to know his address?'

'He didn't say.'

'Did you ask him?'

'Why should I? He said to me "D'you know anyone who wants a gold watch?" and I said – '

'You mean,' interrupted Mr Meldrum, 'that a strange man came up to you in the club and asked you if you wanted to buy a gold watch on the very day you'd gone there to buy one?'

'That's right,' said Mr Briggs, 'a bit of luck, wasn't it?'

'Isn't it the most astonishing bit of luck that's ever happened to you?' asked Mr Meldrum.

'Look, mate, I only made one nicker out of it.'

'You mustn't call counsel "mate",' I said.

'Sorry, guv, no offence.'

'Call him Mr Meldrum,' I said.

'That's his name, is it?'

'Yes, of course,' I said.

'Mr Meldrum. Funny, that. My missus' name was Meldrum.'

'Before you married her, I suppose?' asked Mr Faulkner.

'No, after.'

'After?'

'Yes, she went off with someone else.'

'Do let's get on, Mr Meldrum,' I said.

'Now, Mr Briggs,' Mr Meldrum went on, 'let's get this quite clear. Your story is that, having heard my client say he wants to buy a watch that won't go, you go to your club, and a man you don't know, and whom you've never seen before or since, walks up to you, and without a word spoken by you, asks if you want to buy a gold watch. All that's true, is it?'

'That's for 'im to say,' said Mr Briggs, nodding at me.

'No, Mr Briggs,' I said, 'at the moment it's for you to say. Do you say it's true?'

'Oh, I say it's true, of course,' said Mr Briggs.

'There's no "of course" about it,' said Mr Meldrum. 'If it isn't true, you should say so.'

'What,' said Mr Briggs, 'and be called a liar by both of you?'

'Mr Briggs,' I said, 'this is a much more serious matter than you appear to realise. Sometimes the truth has a nasty way of coming out. Either you or Mr Morris is committing perjury, and one of you ought to be prosecuted for perjury.'

'Ah, but which, my lord?' asked Mr Briggs, 'that's the question, ain't it?'

'This is not a laughing matter, Mr Briggs,' I said, 'as you may very well find out if it transpires that it's you who are telling lies.'

'What should I want to tell lies for?' asked Mr Briggs.

'Perhaps I can answer for you, Mr Briggs,' said Mr Meldrum. 'Would you tell a lie for £50?'

'Less than that,' conceded Mr Briggs.

'So you admit you'd commit perjury for money?'

'Oh no,' said Mr Briggs, 'not perjury. You said would I tell a lie for £50. Well I've often told them for nothing. But not 'ere, not in court, that's different. May my grandmother's soul rot in hell if I tell a lie 'ere.'

'Mr Morris put it a little less dramatically,' I said. 'He said, "if I never speak another word, what I now say is true." Which of you am I to believe?'

'Ah,' said Mr Briggs, 'that's what you're there for, my lord.'

'Mr Faulkner and Mr Meldrum,' I said, addressing counsel, 'what might have been what Mr Carr called a petty squabble has turned out to be something much more serious. I want to assure both of your clients that I shall not hesitate to send the papers to the Director of Public Prosecutions if I think perjury can be proved against one of them.'

And I meant it. Either the plaintiff had invented the watch in order to get more damages from the defendant, or the defendant had persuaded these two witnesses, Briggs and Carr, to tell lies to discredit the plaintiff. Both alternatives were most unlikely. Yet one of them in the end must turn out to be a fact. But which? After Briggs had finished his evidence, I recalled Mr Carr to the witness box.

'I'm sorry to trouble you, Mr Carr,' I said, 'but there's a question I'd like to ask you. You've come here to give evidence because the defendant, Mr Riley, asked you to?'

'I wouldn't have come if I hadn't had a summons,' said Mr Carr.

'Quite so,' I said. 'But what I want to know is how Mr Riley knew you could give this evidence. Has either counsel any objection to my asking this question?' I asked.

Both counsel agreed.

'Then tell me, Mr Carr,' I said, 'why did Mr Riley think you could help him about the case?'

'Because I told him,' said Mr Carr.

'Told him what?'

'About the watch.'

'When?'

'Yesterday.'

'Yesterday!' I said.

'Yes, your honour.'

'Where?'

'In the street.'

'D'you know Mr Riley then?'

'By sight. He comes to my pub sometimes.'

'Go on, Mr Carr,' I said, 'what happened?'

'Well, I saw him in the street and we stopped to have a chat.'

'How did the watch come up?' I asked.

'He's a customer, and you want to be pleasant to them. I didn't really want to stop. I had to think of something to say. Then I thought about the watch. So I told him.'

'What did you tell him?'

'That a man told me he wanted to buy a watch which didn't go.'

'What did he say?'

'At first he didn't take much notice. Then he became interested and asked if I knew the man's name. I said it was Morris. Then he became very interested indeed.'

'And that's how you came into it?' I asked.

'Yes, your honour,' said Mr Carr, 'and I wish I'd kept my ruddy mouth shut.'

Mr Carr was then cross-examined by Mr Meldrum, who asked him as his first question: 'Mr Carr, are you telling his honour that by pure chance Mr Riley learned of your story about the watch yesterday?'

'I am.'

'Had Mr Riley told you that he was being sued by Mr Morris?'

'Not till after I'd told him about the watch.'

'You've been in court while all the evidence has been given in this case.'

'Yes, worse luck,' said Mr Carr.

'How many coincidences were there if your story is true?'

'I haven't counted.'

'But a lot?'

'It seems so.'

'And none the less you say you're telling the truth?' said Mr Meldrum.

'I wish I hadn't,' said Mr Carr.

'How d'you mean?'

'I wish I'd never said a word about it, then I shouldn't be here.'

'I suggest,' said Mr Meldrum, 'that you're simply pretending not to want to be here, and that you conspired with Mr Riley and Mr Briggs to try to discredit my client.'

'Why should I?' said Mr Carr. 'They're both customers, I don't care who wins.'

'I suggest to you,' said Mr Meldrum, 'that Mr Riley is a friend of yours, that he must have told you he had a claim for assault against him, which he was bound to lose, and that he wanted to find some easy way of reducing the damage.'

'You can suggest what you like,' said Mr Carr.

'Isn't Mr Riley a friend of yours?' asked Mr Meldrum.

'He's a customer.'

'Some of your customers are friends as well, aren't they?'

'Yes, of course,' said Mr Carr, 'but Mr Riley isn't particularly.'

'Particularly?' queried Mr Meldrum. 'What does that mean?'

'He's no more a friend than Mr Morris.'

That was all Mr Faulkner wished to ask, and then I recalled Mr Morris back into the witness box. I reminded him that he was still on oath. 'How long d'you say you've had this watch?' I asked.

'Some years, your honour.'

'Did you buy it, or was it a present?'

'My wife gave it to me.'

'Where did she buy it?'

'In Harrogate.'

'Would she know the place where she bought it?'

'I expect so, your honour.'

'Have you had it repaired since she gave it to you?'

'Yes, your honour.'

'Where?'

'In London.'

'D'you know the name and address of the jeweller?'

'I could find it again, your honour.'

'Well, Mr Faulkner and Mr Meldrum,' I said, again addressing counsel, 'hadn't this case better be adjourned for enquiries to be made from both jewellers? Are you agreeable?'

Both counsel agreed. And the case was adjourned for one of them to call the jeweller or jewellers. I made the suggestion because it seemed to me that this would be a way of proving the case conclusively in favour of Mr Morris, or against him. But, of course, both jewellers might have gone out of business, or they might have lost their records. Or they mightn't have kept sufficient records. If that turned out to be the case, what would my decision be? I asked myself. It was most unlikely that the plaintiff would invent the destruction of a watch. He'd behaved very well about his own driving, admitting quite frankly that he was at fault. On the other hand, although the defendant must have been a bad-tempered man, it was equally unlikely that for the sake of reducing the damages, he would take part in what was a conspiracy to defeat the ends of justice. That is what it would have come to. He would have had to be in league with the landlord and the log and dog man. Yet, if this were not the case, there must have been a very odd series of coincidences. Had the log and dog man really met a man who volunteered that he had a gold watch for sale just at the moment when the log and dog man was looking for one? I was concerned, not simply for my own decision, but because this was surely a case where a prosecution for perjury ought to take place if one could be sure who the guilty party was.

Well, the day for the adjourned hearing arrived, and my clerk, Mr Simpson, came in to see me.

'Well, Mr Simpson,' I said, 'what's your bet?'

'I know the answer, your honour,' he said, 'so I can't bet.'

'You know the answer?' I said. 'You should be a judge then instead of me, because I don't.'

'I don't mean that, your honour,' said Mr Simpson. 'They've settled it.'

'They've settled it, have they,' I said. 'That means that one side has given in for fear of a prosecution for perjury. Well, I'm not going to allow that. Ask the local police inspector to come and see me. But first of all, who gave in?'

The clerk told me, and in consequence of that, a visit was paid by Inspector Hughes, not long after, to one of the parties.

From what I subsequently learned, I imagine the conversation between them went something like this. The Inspector introduced himself and asked if he could see Mr George Morris.

'That's me,' said Mr Morris.

'May I come in?' said the Inspector.

Mr Morris invited him in and he sat down.

'Now, Mr Morris,' said the Inspector, 'I'm making enquiries about a claim you brought against Mr Riley for assault.'

'We settled it.'

'Yes, I know. On the terms that you withdrew the action and paid the defendant's costs. That's right, isn't it?'

'Yes,' said Mr Morris, 'that's true.'

'But he struck you in the face.'

'Don't I know it,' said Mr Morris.

'And you were bound to get damages for that assault, weren't you?'

'I certainly should have.'

'Then why did you withdraw the case? For that's what your settlement comes to.'

'I know it must seem funny,' said Mr Morris.

'It isn't funny, but it's certainly strange,' said the Inspector, 'that a man, who's been knocked about and brought the matter to court, should suddenly give it up and pay the other man's costs.'

'Yes,' said Mr Morris, 'it must seem odd to you.'

'Would you care to explain?'

'Oh well,' said Mr Morris, 'I suppose I'd better. It's been on my mind.'

'I think I should warn you,' said the Inspector, 'that anything you do say may be given in evidence if you are prosecuted for perjury.'

'Will I be prosecuted?' asked Mr Morris.

'That's not for me to say,' said the Inspector. 'Now tell me. Why did you invent the story of a damaged watch?'

'I didn't, as a matter of fact,' said Mr Morris.

'Oh really,' said the Inspector, 'I've read all the evidence. You bought that watch from Mr Carr. And you were frightened that the jeweller's records would give you away.'

'How could they have given me away if I never had a watch?' asked Mr Morris. 'It was a cash transaction.'

'Well, you tell me,' said the Inspector.

'All right, I will. That blighter struck me in the face, and he broke a gold watch which my wife had given me.'

'Oh really,' said the Inspector, 'don't waste my time, Mr Morris.'

'I'm not,' said Mr Morris, 'it's absolutely true. It's because my wife *had* given me a watch that the jewellers might have given me away. D'you know what happened? A few days before the trial, I lost the beastly thing. Must have dropped it on a bus or something. I enquired everywhere for it, but it was no good. It seemed too bad that this bloody man should get away with it just because I'd lost it. So I decided to get another instead. It wasn't cheating him. He *had* broken my watch.'

'What an ass you were,' said the Inspector.

'I dare say,' said Mr Morris, 'but, as I'd lost the watch anyway, I couldn't claim damages from the defendant for its being damaged. At least I thought I couldn't, and I just couldn't bear to let him get away with it.'

'It seems to me,' said the Inspector, 'that that's just what you have done.'

It was indeed. And the unfortunate Mr Morris who'd been assaulted, not only lost his case, but he *was* prosecuted for perjury. He pleaded guilty and was fined £100. That certainly was a lesson to him to drive more carefully, if not to tell the truth.

CHAPTER FOUR

Chef's Special

This story is about food and hotels, and, if you are prepared to accept anything which is put before you in the way of food, or bedroom, or service, you will presumably not be very interested in it. I do not intend this remark as a slight upon those who do not much mind what they eat or drink, or how it is served, or how they sleep, for these are matters of individual taste. It would be just as impertinent to criticise a person for not liking music or not liking to look at pictures, or not liking to watch cricket. Conversely, there is no need for people who are interested in food or drink to apologise for being so interested, any more than the music-lover or picture-lover has to apologise. Music tickles the ear, pictures tickle the eye, and food and drink tickle the palate.

At the moment some attempt is perhaps being made to improve the standard of food in English restaurants and hotels and possibly, but less certainly, to improve the service in those places. But, as so many people are content to take what is flung at them, and, as most restaurants and hotels are crowded, there is little incentive to the proprietors and managers of those places to do better than they are doing at present. After all, if without complaint they can serve and be paid for a badly cooked steak with frozen vegetables (through the medium of a waiter, who is not in the least put out if he spills the gravy on the cloth, or even down your back if it gets in the way) why should they try and improve their standard?

But undoubtedly more people are taking an interest in these matters. One has only to look at the large number of food guides and articles in newspapers and magazines on the subject to realise that the gastronomic interest of the public has increased in the last years.

One of the reasons for the low standard of some establishments is because of the very few complaints which people care to make. Most people hate a fuss. And, if complaints are rare, claims for damages for breach of contract brought by a customer against a restaurant or hotel proprietor are even rarer still. But this story is about such a claim, which came in front of me. The plaintiff was a Mr Blandish and he said that he was a journalist and that for the purpose of some of his articles he visited hotels and restaurants and wrote about what he found there without fear, and certainly without favour. According to him, the treatment he received at one particular hotel was at such variance with its prices and its literature that he sued the proprietors for damages for breach of contract. I was intrigued by the case because I admit that I am one of those who take an interest in food. Moreover, it was the only case of its kind which I had ever tried, and I thought it unlikely that I would ever have the opportunity of trying another.

The title of the case was Blandish against the Excelsior Hotel Company Limited. Both sides were represented by counsel, Mr Blandish by the able Mr Benton and the hotel company by an inexperienced young man called Carstairs.

Mr Benton, in opening the case for Mr Blandish, told me that Mr Blandish had no knowledge of this particular hotel before he went there. It was his practice before going to hotels on what might be termed professional visits, to enter into a little correspondence with the hotel to see how they described themselves, and to ascertain the delights which they were offering to prospective visitors. In the course of his opening, Mr Benton produced one of the letters from the Hotel Excelsior which ran as follows: 'This is par excellence the hotel de luxe in the south of England. Here is combined superb food with gracious living in the old style. Our terms are not low, but every farthing is returned with interest in the happiness which we take pleasure in providing for you. The hotel is equivalent to an AA five star hotel in service, comfort and food.'

'The defendants,' said Mr Benton, 'did not explain how every farthing could be returned and the resident proprietors still survive, let alone how they could afford to pay interest as well. But I should make it plain to your honour that this case is not based upon exaggerations of that kind. If the food, or service, or accommodation had been within measurable distance of what it was held out to be, your honour would not now be troubled with the case. My client replied to the defendant's letter as follows: "If your hotel is really substantially in accordance with what you represent it to be, I should like a room with a private bathroom. I need good food, quiet and comfort and am prepared to pay for it."

'The defendants replied that they would be delighted to accommodate my client at the inclusive charge of sixty guineas a week.

'It so happened that my client did want a holiday, and so he booked a room for one week. As your honour will hear, he only stayed for one day, and it is interesting to observe that the defendants are not counterclaiming any damages on the ground that my client booked the room for a week, and only stayed a day. But, whether that is a sign of a guilty conscience, or simply because the defendants find that they can let their rooms so easily, is a matter which your honour will have to judge when you've heard the evidence.'

The plaintiff, Mr Blandish, was then called to give evidence, and the effect of his evidence was this. He said that he arrived at the hotel with two heavy suitcases which he left in his car outside. There was no porter about, so he went up to the reception desk. There he found a young lady painting her nails, and, sitting on a chair not far behind her, a man who was doing a crossword puzzle. Mr Blandish said that first of all he coughed, but, as this produced no effect on the young lady, he said: 'Excuse me.'

'Yes?' said the girl.

'I've just arrived.'

'Have you booked?'

'Yes, the name is Blandish.'

'Sign the register, please. Here's the key. Room thirty-two.'

'What about my baggage?'

'Can't you manage it?'

'No.'

'Is there much?'

'I thought this was a hotel de luxe.'

'Come again,' said the girl. 'If you've any complaints, there's the manager.'

'I only want my luggage taken up,' said Blandish.

'Well, the porter's down the garden.'

'Have you only one porter?'

'The other one's off.'

'On what floor is my room?'

'The third.'

'Perhaps I can go up, and the luggage can follow.'

'The staircase is over there.'

'What about a lift?'

'The lift's out of order.'

'How long will it be out of order?'

'How can I say? I'm not an engineer.'

'Well,' said Blandish, 'can someone come and take my luggage out of the car?'

'Perhaps you'd like *me* to do it,' said the girl.

'No, it's too heavy for a girl.'

'Well, that's the answer to that, then.'

'Can I see the manager, please?'

'I told you, he's over there.'

The plaintiff went on to explain that, after he had said 'Excuse me' twice, in a slightly louder tone on the second occasion, the manager came to life and said: 'Attend to this gentleman, Judy.'

'He's not satisfied,' said the girl.

'Not satisfied with what?' said the manager.

'I simply want my luggage brought in,' said Blandish.

'Can't you manage it?'

'You wrote to me,' said Mr Blandish, 'that this was a hotel de luxe, and your charges certainly justify that expression. I should have thought that someone could have taken in my luggage.'

'If you wait a moment,' said the manager, 'I'll give you a hand.'

'I'm afraid I don't want a hand,' said Blandish. 'I want someone to take in my luggage.'

'Well,' said the manager, 'you must wait for the porter. He's down the garden. You heard the young lady say so.'

'Well, my car's outside in the street,' said Blandish. 'Can I leave it there?'

'Of course you can,' said the manager, 'if you want to be summoned for obstruction. It's a very narrow street, anyone can see that.'

'Well, why can't you come and help take the luggage out now?'

'I've said I would come in a moment,' said the manager, 'if the porter doesn't arrive.'

'Why can't you do it at once?'

'Because I'm busy.'

'Was it you who wrote to me that the hotel was equivalent to an AA five star hotel in service, comfort and food?'

'If I signed it, I wrote it,' said the manager. 'Ah, there's the porter. Ernie, give the gentleman a hand with his luggage, please.'

'I can't,' said the porter, 'I'm busy.'

'When will you be free?' said the manager.

'In half an hour,' said the porter. 'I go off then.'

Mr Blandish explained to me that at that moment a policeman came in and requested him to move his car, and he had to do so. As a result he had to carry his own suitcases several hundred yards back to the hotel.

Eventually he went to his room, which was about twelve feet by ten. It had originally been a little larger, but carved out of it was just enough space for a bath and a lavatory. Eventually he walked downstairs and went into the bar for a drink before dinner. The same young lady who had been in the reception desk was behind the bar, still painting her fingernails and smoking a cigarette.

'Could I have a dry Martini, please?' said Blandish.

'Large or small?'

'Small please. What time is dinner?'

'It's on now,' said the girl. 'If you don't look sharp, you won't get any.'

'But it's only just after half past seven,' said Blandish.

'That's right,' said the girl. 'If you look up there, you'll see dinner is at half past seven.'

The plaintiff said that he then noticed that the girl had poured him out a glass of Italian dry vermouth.

'But I asked for a dry Martini,' he said.

'Can you read?' said the girl, and pointed to the bottle on which were the words 'Martini Dry.'

The plaintiff said that he then tried to explain to the girl the consistency of a dry Martini. To which she replied: 'If you wanted a gin and French, you should have said so. We've no ice anyway.'

'Well, I'll skip the drink,' said Mr Blandish, 'and go into dinner.'

'Wait a moment,' said the girl, 'that will be eight shillings, please.'

'I'm sorry,' said Mr Blandish, 'I'm not paying.'

'Very well,' said the girl, 'it will be on your bill just the same.'

The plaintiff said that he then went into the dining room where he tried to sit at an empty table.

'You can't sit there, sir,' said a waiter. 'It's reserved.' The plaintiff suggested another table. 'That's reserved too. Are you staying in the hotel?'

The plaintiff said that he replied that he was sorry to say that he was.

'Well, the beef's off,' said the waiter. 'Will you have thick, clear or sardine?'

'Would you repeat that?' said Mr Blandish.

'Thick, clear or sardine?' said the waiter.

'Can I see a menu?' said Mr Blandish.

'I'm reading it out to you. Thick, clear or sardine?'

'Is that all there is?'

'Yes, to begin with,' said the waiter. 'Then there's curried mutton to follow or cold ham. The veg is included.'

Once again, Mr Blandish asked to see the manager. About half an hour later he arrived.

'You wanted to see me, sir?' he said.

'Yes, I did. Having regard to the service and the room and the food you are offering, do you consider the statements in your letters were justified?'

'You needn't have come here,' said the manager, 'if you hadn't wanted to.'

'How could I tell what it would be like,' said Mr Blandish, 'apart from what you told me in your letters?'

'Well,' said the manager, 'we've never had any complaints before, and, if you don't like it, you needn't come again.'

'Well, I can only tell you,' said Mr Blandish, 'that I'm not going to pay my bill, and you can sue me for it.'

'We shouldn't dream of suing you for it,' said the manager. 'We shall just hold on to your luggage.'

'So in order to get my luggage,' said Mr Blandish, 'I had to pay the bill. But I told the manager that I should sue and I'm asking for my money back and damages for a most uncomfortable night and a most unpleasant dinner which I shouldn't have experienced but for what the defendants had written in their letter. I may add that I could have cooked a far better dinner myself.'

Mr Blandish was then cross-examined by counsel for the defendants, but, as Mr Carstairs hardly knew the rudiments of cross-examination, it is not surprising that the plaintiff's evidence was not shaken. The defendants then started to call their evidence. And the first witness was the resident manager of the Excelsior Hotel. His name was Thomas Cutworthy.

I had been impressed with the evidence of Mr Blandish. He seemed a truthful and accurate witness. Moreover I myself had had some bad experiences in hotels and restaurants, and I may have been consciously or unconsciously slightly biased against the defendants in consequence. Of course judges shouldn't be biased. But, as we are only human beings, it must sometimes happen that we are, even if we don't appreciate it ourselves. I certainly was prepared to make some pretty scathing remarks about the defendants, if, when I'd heard the whole of the evidence, I was satisfied that the plaintiff's case was true. I was quite ready for Mr Cutworthy to make various excuses of a kind I'd heard before – about difficulties of getting staff, and all that sort of thing. I also expected that some of the plaintiff's evidence would be contradicted, but by and large I felt that the picture painted by the plaintiff would be likely to stick, even after the defendants had called all their evidence. In consequence, I was wholly unprepared for Mr Cutworthy's version of the story.

'Well, Mr Cutworthy,' asked Mr Carstairs, 'what d'you say about the plaintiff's evidence in this matter?'

'What do I say?' said Mr Cutworthy. 'I say that I think he must have gone to a different hotel.'

'D'you mean that?' I asked.

'Certainly, your honour,' said Mr Cutworthy. 'I've been to the sort of establishment which the plaintiff has described. It's nothing like mine. For example, I've brought one of our menus to show your honour. You'll see from this that even the most particular customer has a wide and varied choice. In fact, I heartily agree, your honour, with almost everything the plaintiff has said. If we'd treated him as he described, he would have been fully entitled to make the complaints which he has made.

The conversations he says he had with me are pure inventions as far as I am concerned.'

'Do you say that he never came to your hotel at all?' I asked.

'We have indeed got the registration of a Mr Blandish on the day that he said he stayed there,' said Mr Cutworthy, 'but either what he says is almost entirely a complete fabrication, or he's mixed up our hotel with some other hotel at which he stayed on a different occasion.'

'Well,' I said, 'this is extremely odd. Mr Benton, I don't believe your client, when in the witness box, actually identified Mr Cutworthy. Don't you think he'd better be recalled at once, in case there has been some mistake about it?'

So Mr Blandish was recalled into the witness box and was asked to look at Mr Cutworthy and say if he was the man whom he'd described as being the manager of the hotel where he stayed on the night in question.

'Yes,' said Mr Blandish, and then paused. 'I think so,' he added.

'You *think* so?' I asked.

'Well, your honour,' said Mr Blandish, 'I only saw him on one day and that was some little time ago.'

'But your name is in the visitors' book,' I said.

'It's in the visitors' book of a lot of hotels,' said Blandish.

'Any in the same neighbourhood?' I said.

'Quite possibly. But, your honour, I don't think there is any doubt that this is the man. I must admit, however, I haven't got a good memory for faces, and I've been asked on my oath if I can swear positively that he is the man. Naturally I want to be careful about this.'

'You are quite right to be careful,' I said, 'but you described in detail your first entrance to the hotel and what you saw and heard. Have you any doubt about what you've told us?'

'None at all, your honour,' said Blandish.

'Have you any doubt about the position of the hotel?'

'No, your honour.'

'Then,' I said, 'the only thing you are not absolutely certain about is whether the gentleman standing in the witness box is the manager of that hotel?'

'That is so, your honour.'

'But,' I said, 'he swears that he is.'

'He also swears,' said Mr Blandish, 'that the conversations to which I referred didn't take place. One of us must be wrong. Perhaps there has been a change of managers.'

I went into that question but it became plain that Mr Cutworthy claimed that he was quite definitely the resident manager of the hotel on the date when Mr Blandish said he'd visited it. Mr Blandish was then asked if he recognised the young lady sitting in the third row of the seats behind counsel.

'Is that the young lady who was in the reception desk and behind the bar?' asked Mr Carstairs.

'This one seems better-looking, if I may say so,' said Mr Blandish.

'But,' I said, 'do they look about the same?'

'Well,' said Mr Blandish, 'this young lady is really very attractive, I don't think the other was.'

'Perhaps it's what she did that made her look less attractive?' I said. 'In the course of many years I've noticed that a woman who looks quite plain when you first look at her, begins to look extremely attractive when she says nice things about you. And to a lesser extent, vice versa.'

'Well, Mr Blandish,' said Mr Carstairs, 'is it the same girl, or is it not?'

71

'I can't swear one way or the other.'

'Have you more or less doubt about her than you have about Mr Cutworthy?' I asked.

'More doubt, your honour.'

'Let us be clear,' said Mr Carstairs, 'that we are speaking about the same place? Mr Blandish, will you be kind enough to look at the menu which Mr Cutworthy has produced?'

The menu was taken by the usher over to Mr Blandish. 'Do you dispute,' said Mr Carstairs, 'that that was the menu which was placed in front of you?'

'I've already told you,' said Mr Blandish, 'that no menu was placed in front of me. But I did see a card in the waiter's hand. This menu is six times as large as that. This menu is the kind you might expect to find in one of the most exclusive London restaurants.'

'Then you would approve of a place,' said Mr Carstairs, 'which had a menu like this?'

'Not necessarily, by any means,' said Mr Blandish. 'On the whole, the places in the country which have these huge menus are pretentious and bad. They don't get a call for half the food which is shown there, and either they can't supply it when asked, or it's been frozen and kept in a deep-freeze for months.'

'Do you say,' persisted Mr Carstairs, 'that this is not the menu of the hotel you've been talking about?'

'All I say,' said Mr Blandish, 'is that such a menu was not produced to me, and I did not see it in the waiter's hands.'

'What about the wine list?' asked Mr Carstairs.

'In view of everything else,' said Mr Blandish, 'I didn't bother to ask for one.'

'Have a look at this then, please.'

A wine list was then handed to the witness. Mr Blandish looked at it.

'Is this supposed to be the wine list of the hotel that I've been talking about?'

'It certainly is,' said counsel.

'Well, all I can say,' said Mr Blandish, 'is this. I do not believe for one moment that the hotel which treated me in the way I was treated, which supplied the food with which I was supplied, and where the girl in the bar didn't know what was meant by a dry Martini, I do not believe that such a hotel would have a wine list like this.'

'How would you describe *this* wine list?' I asked.

'Very good indeed,' said Mr Blandish. 'Of course without trying the wine, I can't say whether it comes up to the wine list, but from a casual glance, I should say it was one of the best wine lists that I've ever seen. And if you'll give me a moment, your honour,' he added, 'I'll say something about the prices.' He paused. 'They seem extremely reasonable. Of course anyone can print a wine list. Even in good places you sometimes find that the wine on the wine list is not available. In bad places this happens very frequently, particularly with regard to the vintages.'

Mr Blandish then left the witness box, and Mr Cutworthy went on with his evidence. He was asked what he said about Mr Blandish's further evidence.

'I simply don't understand it,' he said. 'I know the sort of place which Mr Blandish has described, and I sympathise with him on the treatment he received. But it simply cannot have been my place. Take only a tiny example. It's quite true that one of my receptionists (and I have three) one of my receptionists does occasionally help behind the bar if the barman is off duty. But she knows her job extremely well. She makes as good a dry Martini as any barman that I know. We get a lot of Americans coming to our hotel, your honour, and they are delighted with our dry Martinis. Mr Blandish must have been talking about a different place.'

I was extremely puzzled. And, when counsel suggested that they should all visit Mr Cutworthy's hotel, it seemed to me that it was the only practicable solution to the problem. Mr Cutworthy then suggested through his counsel that we should all lunch there at his expense. I was prepared to lunch there with both parties and their counsel, but I said that I insisted on paying a proper sum for myself.

So the case was adjourned and we all went down to the Excelsior Hotel. It was a very different place from that described by Mr Blandish. And he agreed that everything, service, food and wine was superb, and that the price, though high, was not at all unreasonable for what was provided. He further agreed that the place came fully up to the statements made in the letters written to him before he went there. After lunch, we returned to the court. Mr Blandish was invited to go into the witness box again. He stood in the witness box for a full half minute without saying anything at all. Eventually I said: 'You seem at a loss for words.'

'I am, your honour.'

'You agree, then,' I said, 'that, what must have been obvious to all of us, this was one of the most splendid lunches you've ever attended.'

'Absolutely.'

'Then,' I said, 'you must answer this question. Is the hotel we went to the same place that you described to me this morning?'

'I just don't know what to say, your honour. I could have sworn it was, and yet it can't be. And yet again, I registered there, and they still have my registration. And if it's not the place I gave evidence about this morning, where is that place? I can't have imagined it. I can only suggest that either as a result of my visit, or for some other reason, the proprietors or manager of this hotel suddenly had a change of heart, and completely altered the nature of the hotel. But I must admit, I shouldn't have thought it possible for the man whom I saw to perform such a miracle of change.'

'What about the young lady?' I asked.

'As to that,' said Mr Blandish, 'I can only say that her Martinis are excellent, and that her behaviour to us was the very reverse of what I experienced from the girl who attended to me. But undoubtedly they do look rather alike. On the other hand, I find it very difficult to think that such a metamorphosis can have taken place in her case either. It was the attitude of mind, your honour. Both the manager and the girl were surly-minded, and behaved accordingly. This gentleman and this girl are completely different people. Actors on the stage can play all sorts of different parts, but I can't conceive it being done to such an extent in real life.'

After all the evidence had been given, I invited counsel on both sides to my private room.

'This is one of the most puzzling cases I've ever tried,' I said. 'As at present advised, I believe both your clients, yet they can't both be right. I don't think the explanation can be that there was a change of heart on the part of Mr Cutworthy and his staff. I think Mr Blandish is right when he says it's an attitude of mind. To be quite frank with you, I have no idea what the explanation is.'

Counsel admitted to me that they too were equally in the dark. I then suggested that, in view of the excellent lunch which they'd had at the expense of Mr Cutworthy, it might be possible for them to come to a solution of the case which would not involve a slur upon anyone. And eventually, after some little bargaining between counsel, a settlement was reached. The action was withdrawn, and each party paid its own costs. Which meant that both Mr Blandish and the Excelsior Hotel Company were each liable to their own solicitors for about £100. So in effect each party had lost. Only the lawyers had gained. Nevertheless it seemed to me the only practicable solution to the matter and I was glad that I did not have to give a decision myself.

But for some time I remained extremely puzzled about it. I was used to cases where one party swore it was black, and the other party swore it was white, and the answer was grey. I was used to cases where one party swore it was black, and the other swore it was white, and the answer was black or white, or even orange, but this case didn't fit into any category. I wondered about it for days, and, although after some time other problems and events drove thoughts of it out of my mind, my brain still went back to it from time to time and I tried to solve the mystery. But always without success.

Then, one day, during a weekend when I was passing near the hotel in question, I decided to pay it a visit. The place was crowded. There is no doubt that in consequence of the excellent way in which it was run, coupled with the very great publicity which the case had attracted – 'The Phantom Hotel Case' it was called by some newspapers – the hotel had attracted a huge clientele. I managed to get a table for dinner but only because one had been cancelled. I found that everything was as perfect as it could be. When I had finished, I asked the waiter if I could see the manager. I wanted to congratulate him.

'The manager, sir?' said the waiter. 'I hope there's nothing wrong.'

'Oh no,' I said, 'on the contrary.'

'Very good, sir,' said the waiter. 'He'll be with you in a moment.'

A few minutes later the manager arrived. But it was not Mr Cutworthy, it was Mr Blandish. The case was a mystery to me no longer.

CHAPTER FIVE

Retrial

As a County Court judge I did not try criminal cases. But, oddly enough, in the story which I am going to tell you, that's in effect what I had to do. As a barrister I should not have liked to have had a criminal practice. Of course there are interesting cases from time to time, but most of them have a certain sameness. You would soon get used to the following dialogue:

Counsel: Did you steal it?

Old Lag: What should I want to steal it for?

It's very odd the way even the most hardened criminal often tries to avoid giving the direct negative answer when it would be a lie. He prefers to parry the question by saying, 'what should I want to steal it for?' He funks the lie direct. 'What should I want to steal it for?' he says. And of course it isn't only old lags who do this. Quite respectable people sometimes try to avoid telling a lie by this subterfuge.

I must now explain how it came about that in a County Court I had to try what was in effect a criminal case. Or rather I had to retry it. There is a principle of the English Law that it is in the interests of the State that there should be an end of litigation. But, curiously enough, there is one branch of law in this country where that principle has not been applied.

If Henry Brown commits a crime, or rather is convicted of committing a crime, and subsequently someone states that Brown has committed the crime, it is open to Brown to bring an action in the Civil Courts for libel on the ground that in fact he was innocent. And in that case, if the person who is sued seeks to justify the statement that the plaintiff has committed the crime, the whole matter will have to be gone into again. And not only that. It will not be evidence against the defendant that he has been convicted of the crime which is alleged against him. So a person who has been convicted can in fact use the Civil Courts to try and establish his innocence, even though he has failed on appeal, even to the House of Lords. Not so very long ago this was done successfully by Mr Alfred Hinds. Although he had been convicted and failed in his appeals to the Court of Criminal Appeal, none the less he came before a Civil jury and they found that he was innocent.

It was a similar case to that which came in front of me. Mr Elgar, the plaintiff, was a schoolmaster, and he'd been dismissed by the Crockston Borough Council from his employment by them on the ground that it was a term in his contract that, if he did anything discreditable that brought him into disrepute, he might be dismissed without notice.

Now Mr Elgar had been convicted of shoplifting, and the magistrate who convicted him, in spite of his protestations of innocence, said that it was a mean little theft, and fined him £2. Mr Elgar appealed, but his appeal was dismissed with costs. He then wrote to the Home Secretary, but with no satisfactory result from his point of view. In due course he received a letter to the effect that the

Home Secretary had carefully considered all the material which Mr Elgar had put before him, but regretted that he could see no reason to advise Her Majesty to interfere with the conviction.

But Mr Elgar still had one card to play, and he played it in front of me. It is true that no one had libelled him, because a contemporaneous report of his conviction before the magistrate is privileged. No one said that he was guilty, they merely reported what had happened in the court, and, of course, it is so important in the public interest that cases should be allowed to be reported that you can do so with impunity, provided you don't add anything to the facts which occurred in court. And, of course, provided you don't make any unfair comment about them. But though no one had libelled Mr Elgar, the Borough Council had dismissed him without notice, relying upon the term in the contract to which I have referred. Accordingly it was open to Mr Elgar to bring an action against the Crockston Borough Council for wrongful dismissal. If they had wanted to dismiss him for no particular reason such as the one that was alleged against him, they would have had to have given him at least a term's notice. I feel sure that, if they had realised the danger of dismissing him without notice, they would have given him the full notice to which he was entitled, so as to avoid the proceedings which in fact were brought against them. Whether he was entitled to such notice or whether he wasn't, it was obviously in the interests of the ratepayers that litigation of this kind should be avoided, if possible.

But, as soon as Mr Elgar's appeal from his conviction had been dismissed, the Council, acting as they thought in accordance with their duties, dismissed him peremptorily. This was a great advantage to Mr Elgar because it gave him the opportunity of having his whole case retried in front of me.

When the case came on, Mr Elgar appeared in person. He did this, he said, because he considered that it was the only way in which he could get justice.

'The lawyers who've so far represented me,' he said, 'no doubt did their best, but they didn't seem to realise how vital the case was for me. Indeed, one of them said to me that, as the magistrate only fined me £2, it showed that it wasn't such a very serious offence. If he'd only fined me one shilling, your honour,' went on Mr Elgar, 'that fine would have been the ruin of my career and my life.'

I told Mr Elgar that I was not in the least concerned with the magistrate's decision.

'It would be idle to pretend,' I said, 'that I am not aware of it, and of the fact that your appeal was dismissed. But other people gave those decisions, and they're nothing to do with me. I shall approach the facts completely afresh, and shall decide which way I think proper. If it's any help to you,' I added, 'I should tell you that I've before now decided quite differently from a magistrate in a motoring case. For example, I've found that a person who was convicted of careless driving was not negligent at all.'

Mr Elgar said that he was very glad to hear that.

'On the other hand,' I went on, 'it's only fair to tell you, Mr Elgar, that I've also decided that a man who was acquitted by the magistrate was guilty of negligent driving. I should also tell you,' I said, 'that I didn't read your case carefully, and the details, as far as I can remember, are not known to me. I suggest that you go into the witness box and tell me your case in full.'

So Mr Elgar went into the witness box and took the oath. He took it very solemnly and with some feeling, and at the end of it he said: 'I hope that this time I'll be believed. It's a terrible thing to tell the truth and not to be believed.'

'Tell me what happened,' I said.

'Well,' said Mr Elgar, 'it was in the holidays and I'd gone for a walk, and I passed the shop where they said I stole the things. Then I suddenly remembered that there was something I wanted that I'd seen in the window. I went back and into the shop. It was rather warm there so I took off my overcoat and put it over my arm.'

'How long did you stay in the shop?' I asked.

'About half an hour, your honour. Is it likely that I would have done that, your honour, if I were going to steal things there, or if I'd already stolen them? I walked round the shop and there were quite a number of things which interested me. One or two I decided to buy. I bought a cheap fountain pen for seven and sixpence, and two memo blocks, and I paid for them and got a receipt. I put the pen and the memo pads in my jacket pocket. I ought to have told your honour that a few days previously I'd bought a couple of pencils elsewhere.'

'Where did you buy them?' I asked.

'I'm not sure. It might have been one of two shops. They were small pencils with india rubber attached to them, and they were a well-known brand. When I'd finished looking round, I went out of the shop. I'd walked about twenty yards when a man touched me on the shoulder. He told me that he was the store detective. I asked him what he wanted. "I believe you've taken certain articles from that shop which you've not paid for," he said, "and I shall be obliged if you'll come back with me to the shop." I said I'd never heard anything so absurd in all my life. He repeated his request for me to come back to the shop, and asked me if I objected. "I certainly do," I said, "it's a ridiculous suggestion to make." "I'm afraid I must ask you to accompany me," he said. "And if I refuse?" "I'm afraid I shall call a policeman." "This may do me a tremendous amount of harm," I said, "I'm a schoolmaster." "I'm very sorry, sir," he said, "but, if what you say is correct, it won't do you any harm at all. Only the manager and I and a couple of assistants know anything about it. If we're satisfied that you're innocent, we'll let you go and apologise."

'I could see there was no point in arguing about the matter, so I went back to the shop and into the manager's office. Then they started questioning me. First of all they asked me if I'd mind emptying my pockets. I asked why on earth I should. "I should have thought," said the store detective, "you'd have wanted to, sir. If you've nothing incriminating on you, it will help to clear you." "Do you ask every member of the public to empty his pockets," I said, "to see if he's got anything incriminating on him?" "Of course not, sir. But I have some evidence that you've taken things without paying for them. What did you buy here, sir?" "A pen and a couple of memo pads, and I've got receipts for them." "Nothing else?" "No." "You're quite sure you bought nothing else?" "Yes, I'm quite sure." "Then if you've bought nothing else, you've paid for nothing else?" "Of course I haven't," I said. "I've paid for what I've bought."

'They then asked me to turn out my pockets, and with some reluctance I agreed. It was a great indignity, but I didn't see any alternative. The manager and the store detective were both present. There was nothing in my pockets which interested them. Then the store detective asked me about my overcoat, and whether there was anything in that. I said I'd see. I put my hand in the pockets and brought out two pencils and two more memo pads. The store detective then pointed out that the two pencils were exactly similar to pencils in a tray in the shop, and he also pointed out that I'd only paid for two memo pads, and not for four. "Where did these two memo pads, and these pencils come from?" he asked. "I don't know where the memo pads came from," I said. "The pencils I bought at another shop, and I paid for them." I was asked if I had a receipt, and I said I hadn't, and that I'd bought them some days ago. The store detective then said that both the memo pads and the pencils were exactly the same as the memo pads and pencils on sale in the shop in which we were. I in turn pointed out that they were exactly the same as pencils and memo pads in hundreds of other shops. I was then asked for the name of the shop where I'd bought the pencils, and I repeated that I couldn't say exactly which it was, and that it was one of two shops. The detective then again asked me how I accounted for the memo pads, and I said that I couldn't. "I ought to tell you," said the store detective, "that there are memo pads and pencils missing from the trays in this shop and they have not been paid for. You have two of the memo pads, and two of the pencils, and you haven't paid for them, and you agree that you weren't going to pay for them. I'm afraid I shall have to send for the police."

'So the police were sent for, and I was charged with stealing, and released on bail. And that's all there is to it, your honour. It's a gross miscarriage of justice. The defendants dismissed me, and I went to see the chairman of the governors. He told me that there was nothing more he could do about it.'

'Tell me what took place between you,' I said.

'I pointed out that mistakes are made from time to time, and the chairman said he was aware of that. "But the Home Secretary's considered your case too, and refused to interfere," he said. "How can we?" "Because I ask you to,"

I said. "Look at me, don't I look as though I were telling the truth?" "I'm afraid," said the chairman, "that I'm not a judge of that, we have to rely on the courts." I said to him: "What about Adolph Beck who spent years in prison as a result of an unjust conviction? Why have you got to follow the courts' decision? If you believe me, you can say that they're wrong. After all, the courts are only men." But the chairman repeated that there was nothing more that he could do about it. In consequence every decent school is now barred to me. I'm bringing this claim not for the money, but to re-establish my character. All I want is for you to say that I didn't steal anything. I'm told you have the power to do that, and I ask you to do it.'

I then asked counsel for the Borough Council, Mr Benton, if he would like to cross-examine, and he rose to do so.

'Mr Elgar,' he asked, 'this episode took place in June. D'you usually wear an overcoat in the summer?'

'Like everyone else,' said Mr Elgar, 'sometimes I do and sometimes I don't.'

'You give the impression of being a neat and tidy person, if I may say so,' went on Mr Benton. 'Was your overcoat also neat and tidy?'

'It looked respectable, I suppose.'

'What about the pockets. Were they neat and tidy?'

'They were just pockets.'

'Yes, I know,' said Mr Benton, 'but there are pockets and pockets. For example, some people stuff newspapers and all sorts of things into their pockets, and they bulge. Other people keep them much more like they were when they were new. Which do you do, Mr Elgar?'

'I didn't stuff newspapers into them.'

'Or apples or oranges?' asked Mr Benton.

'No,' said Mr Elgar, 'nor bananas.'

'How do you account for the two memo pads being in one of your overcoat pockets?'

'Someone must have put them there,' said Mr Elgar.

'Before you were detained by the store detective, or after?'

'Oh, I don't suggest they were planted on me.'

'Then you say they must have been put into your pocket by someone else before you left the shop?'

'I suppose so.'

'What alternative is there?'

'I can't think of any.'

'If your pockets were well pressed, not bulgy I mean, and you were holding the overcoat over your arm all the time, how could anyone else have put the memo pads in?'

'Well, if I could put them in, someone else could put them in.'

'Mr Elgar,' said Mr Benton, 'it's quite a different thing for the owner of a coat who was carrying it to slip two memo pads into his pocket.'

'I don't like the way you said "slip",' said Mr Elgar.

'Very well, Mr Elgar, I'm sorry. I'll say "to put" two memo pads into his pocket. It's quite another thing for a stranger to do that without the owner of the coat being aware of it.'

'What is your question?' asked Mr Elgar.

'Don't you think it would be a difficult thing to do?'

'I don't know if it's easy or difficult,' said Mr Elgar, 'but it must have happened.'

'Unless,' said Mr Benton, 'you put them in yourself.'

'Well, I didn't.'

'Why do you think someone else should want to put two memo pads into your pocket?'

'I've no idea.'

'Well, try to think, Mr Elgar. You don't suggest that some stranger, looking at you, said to himself: "Well there's a poor fellow who could do with two memo pads, I'll slip a couple into his pocket".'

'This may be funny to you, Mr Benton,' said Mr Elgar, 'but it means everything to me.'

'I'm not trying to be funny,' said Mr Benton, 'I'm simply trying to examine the possibilities. I want to give you the opportunity of saying how and why someone else put these things into your pocket.'

'It's a strange world,' said Mr Elgar, 'and people do strange things. There are lunatics about. All I say is I didn't take them.'

'And now for the pencils,' said Mr Benton. 'You agree there was a tray in the shop of pencils just like this?'

'Of course there was, as in many other shops.'

'Doesn't it strike you as a little odd, Mr Elgar, that on the same occasion when some stranger for no known reason puts two of the shop's memo pads into your pocket, by coincidence you should also have in your overcoat pocket two pencils exactly like pencils which had been on sale in the shop, and which were missing?'

'It's a little odd, but so are a lot of things. I'd bought these pencils elsewhere.'

'Was there anybody with you when you bought them?'

'Yes, as a matter of fact there was.'

'Is the witness here today?'

'Yes, she is.'

'Is she a relative or friend of yours?'

'She's just an acquaintance.'

That was all Mr Benton wished to ask Mr Elgar, and a few moments later he called his witness, Mrs Lydia Long. Now Mr Elgar struck me as a perfectly ordinary normal person, but his witness, Mrs Lydia Long, was something very different. When I asked for her full name, she seemed reluctant to give it. As an explanation she said that her father was rather odd.

'Never mind your father, Mrs Long,' I said, 'I just want to know your full name.'

'D'you mean that?' she asked.

'Of course I mean it,' I said.

'Well,' said Mrs Long, 'you're in for a shock. I have twenty-five names. They had to issue a special birth certificate. I'm afraid I haven't brought it with me, but I could get it, and they're such odd ones. Some of them are places, some are things, some are ordinary names.'

'I see, madam,' I said. 'What are you generally known as?'

'Oh, I'm generally known as – ' she began. 'D'you mean by the people in the street?'

'I mean,' I said, 'by your friends and relatives and tradesmen and so on.'

'Well, it varies a great deal,' said Mrs Long. 'I have a lot of nieces and nephews, and of course they call me Auntie.'

'Tradesmen, then,' I asked.

'Oh, tradesmen. Most of them down my way call me "dear".'

'Very well,' I said, 'we shall call you Mrs Lydia Long.'

'I could give you the other names if you really wanted them, but it does take rather a time.'

'No, it doesn't matter,' I said.

'You see words like "Tabernacle" come into it.'

'Let's forget about the name, Mrs Long,' I said. 'Now tell me, please, what street d'you live in?'

'Well, it isn't actually a street, I'm afraid.'

'What is your address, please?'

'I'll give you a card,' said Mrs Long.

'Would you please say it out loud.'

Mrs Long then shouted: 'Hassocks, Denby Place, SW4.'

'There's no need to shout,' I said.

'But you asked me to,' said Mrs Long.

I realised that Mrs Long required rather gentle handling. I asked her if she remembered reading about Mr Elgar being prosecuted.

'I should say I did,' she said. 'You could have knocked me down. I didn't believe it. I thought it must be somebody else. He's such a nice man. I know he'd never do anything like that. I'd trust him with anything of mine. He's a good man. You can see it in him, and I know a good man when I see one. You're a good man, your honour,' she added, 'I'd trust you anywhere too. Not as much as Mr Elgar, of course, but near enough. I've known him longer, you see.'

'D'you remember,' I said, 'going into a shop with Mr Elgar a short time before he was prosecuted?'

'That's what I've come to say,' she said.

'Very well, Mr Elgar,' I said, 'would you like to go on examining the witness. And try not to put the words into her mouth.'

So Mr Elgar took up the examination.

'You remember,' he said, 'coming into a shop with me, a stationer's?'

'Oh, very well,' said Mrs Long. 'As it happens, I remember what we were talking about. Of all the stupid things I said to you – '

But I intervened.

'We don't want to hear the conversation, Mrs Long.'

'Oh do, it would amuse you.'

'Behave yourself please, Mrs Long.'

'I might just as well not have come,' said Mrs Long.

'Mr Elgar,' I said, 'please ask your next question.'

'Did I buy any pencils?' he asked.

'Yes, certainly you did.'

'Look at these pencils please, Mrs Long.'

I asked the usher to take them to the witness.

'These are the pencils,' said Mrs Long.

'Those are the pencils you saw me buy?' repeated Mr Elgar.

'I wondered why you wanted two,' said Mrs Long.

'And those are the pencils?' repeated Mr Elgar.

'They are the pencils,' said Mrs Long.

'That is all I wish to ask, your honour,' said Mr Elgar.

I invited Mr Benton to cross-examine.

'Mrs Long,' was his first question, 'is there any mark on the pencils?'

'Mark? How d'you mean?'

'Is there any mark on the pencils?'

'You said that before.'

'I know I did, but you didn't answer.'

'I certainly did. I said what d'you mean by a mark?'

'By a mark I mean a mark.'

'What kind of a mark?' asked Mrs Long.

'Any kind of mark.'

'Well, I don't know what you're talking about, I'm sure.'

I intervened.

'All Mr Benton wants to know,' I said, 'is if you can see any mark on either of those pencils.'

'Perhaps you can, your honour,' said Mrs Long.

'Can you?' I asked.

'Nothing special.'

'Then,' said Mr Benton, 'how can you say those are the pencils?'

'Because I'm on oath,' said Mrs Long. 'I've sworn to tell the truth, and those are the pencils.'

'Are those the two pencils which you saw Mr Elgar buy?' asked Mr Benton.

'Now you've got it,' said Mrs Long.

'The exact same pencils?' persisted Mr Benton.

'Now you're not starting all over again,' said Mrs Long.

'Are they the exact same pencils?' said Mr Benton.

'Isn't it in the "Hunting of the Snark",' said Mrs Long, 'that someone says, "What I tell you three times is true"?'

Again I intervened.

'Mrs Long,' I said, 'I must kindly ask you once more to behave yourself.'

'You said that before, your honour,' said Mrs Long. 'I thought I was. I'm wearing a hat and a decent length skirt, what should I have done?'

'You should answer the questions properly.'

'I thought I had.'

'The "Hunting of the Snark",' I said, 'has got nothing to do with the questions Mr Benton is asking you.'

'You know it, then, your honour?'

'Mr Benton, would you ask the question again, please,' I said.

'Are those two pencils the exact same pencils which you saw Mr Elgar buy on the occasion to which you have referred?' asked Mr Benton.

'If I answer you this time,' said Mrs Long, 'will you promise not to ask again?'

'You mustn't talk to counsel like that, Mrs Long,' I said. 'It's for me to decide whether counsel asks the question too often, and I'll protect you if he does.'

'You'll protect me, your honour?' said Mrs Long.

'Yes.'

'That'll be something to remember,' she said.

'Well, Mrs Long, are they the pencils?' asked Mr Benton.

'They are. They are, they are, they are. Is that enough times?'

'Those pencils, madam,' said Mr Benton, 'are made in hundreds of thousands. How can you say that the two pencils in front of you are the very pencils which Mr Elgar bought, and not two like them.'

'That's what I mean,' said Mrs Long.

'You mean the pencils in front of you are like the ones you saw Mr Elgar buy?'

'Oh dear, oh dear, oh dear,' said Mrs Long, 'haven't I just told you so?'

'What you said several times, madam,' said Mr Benton, 'is that these are the actual pencils, not just like the actual pencils, but the actual pencils.'

'How can I tell one from another?' said Mrs Long, 'they're all the same.'

'So, Mrs Long,' said Mr Benton, 'you saw Mr Elgar buy two pencils. Did you by any chance see what he did with them?'

'What he did with them?' queried Mrs Long.

'What he did with them,' repeated Mr Benton.

'Yes,' said Mrs Long, 'I heard you the first time. But what d'you expect him to do with them? I know some people eat pencils, but you don't expect him to start doing that as soon as he'd bought them?'

'Was there a rubber on the end?' I asked.

'I believe there was,' said Mrs Long, 'but you could take the whole thing off if you wanted to have a bite.'

'Did you see whether the pencils were put in a bag before he took them away?' asked Mr Benton.

'It would have been a waste of time if they were.'

'But were they?'

'You must ask him that. After all, he was buying them and he might have wanted a bag too.'

'Had he got an overcoat?'

'Really,' said Mrs Long, 'I don't own the man. How do I know what he'd got? You'll ask me the colour of his shirt next. He's an ordinary man dressed in the ordinary way, and he bought two ordinary pencils.'

'And had he got two ordinary pockets in his ordinary overcoat?' asked Mr Benton.

'I can't keep this up,' said Mrs Long, 'but I should imagine so.'

'But what he did with the pencils you can't say?'

'Can't I?'

'Well, can you?'

'Can't I what?'

'I said "can you".'

'And I said "Can't I?" '

'Mrs Long,' I said, 'I don't know whether you are trying to be funny or have some kind of game with counsel, but I must warn you that I can't allow that sort of thing in this court.'

'I wouldn't allow it myself in your place,' said Mrs Long. 'What's the good of being up there if you can't make people behave themselves?'

'I take the hint, Mrs Long, and if this occurs again, I shall fine you for contempt of court.'

'I shan't come here again in a hurry,' said Mrs Long.

'Mrs Long,' I said, 'if you go on trying to be funny, first of all I shall fine you, and then I shall send you to prison.'

'I knew I was wrong to come,' said Mrs Long.

'Go on, please, Mr Benton,' I said.

'Madam,' said Mr Benton, 'did you see what Mr Elgar did with the two pencils which you saw him buy?'

'He took them away with him.'

'In his hand or in his pocket, or how?'

'I've already told you, that's for him to say,' said Mrs Long.

'Very well then,' said Mr Benton. 'Now, Mrs Long, would you tell me something else. What day of the week was this on?'

'I don't keep a diary,' said Mrs Long, 'and if I had, I shouldn't have written in it. Even Pepys wouldn't have written "saw Mr Elgar buy two pencils, mighty strange".'

'When were you aware that Mr Elgar had been arrested?'

'When I saw it in the papers.'

'Are you able to swear positively that the day when you saw him buy the two pencils was a few days before he was arrested?'

'That is what I'm here to swear.'

'That may be, madam,' said Mr Benton, 'but how d'you know the day?'

'Well, today's Thursday, isn't it?'

'Yes, it is,'

'Well, I got that right, why shouldn't I have got the other right?'

'Well, what day of the week was it, madam?' said Mr Benton. 'Was it Thursday, or Monday, or what other day?'

'It was a few days before he was arrested.'

'How d'you know?'

'Because he told me so.'

'When did he tell you so?'

'Good gracious me, is this going on much longer?'

'When did he tell you?'

'I really couldn't say.'

'Was it on the day when you read about the case?'

'No, I didn't see him that day. Anyway he was locked up, wasn't he?'

'He was on bail as a matter of fact, madam,' said Mr Benton.

'You can't tell by looking at a man whether he's on bail or not,' said Mrs Long.

'Was it today that he told you?'

'No.'

'Was it yesterday?'

'I didn't see him yesterday.'

'He could have told you on the telephone.'

'I haven't got a telephone.'

'So it was on some day between the day of his arrest, and yesterday?'

'That's what you say.'

'There isn't any other possibility, is there?' said Mr Benton.

'Well, if you're satisfied, so am I,' said Mrs Long. 'Can I go home now?'

'I'm afraid,' I said, 'you'll have to stay here until the end of the case.'

'When will that be?'

'I don't know, but you're prolonging the trial very considerably.'

'I'm not used to courts,' said Mrs Long.

'That is all I wish to ask,' said Mr Benton.

'Mrs Long,' said Mr Elgar, 'you're quite sure you saw me leave that shop with the two pencils in my pocket?'

'That's what you wanted me to say,' said Mrs Long, 'isn't it?'

'Yes.'

'Well, I've said it, haven't I?'

'Thank you, Mrs Long,' said Mr Elgar, 'I've no more witnesses, your honour.'

The defendants then called their evidence. First they called the shop manager, Mr Robinson. He hadn't seen anything happen himself, but as the result of what he was told, he counted up the pencils and the memo pads, and he found that there were five pencils missing, and four memo pads. And he said that the pads and pencils were exactly the same as those found in Mr Elgar's coat pocket. He was then questioned by Mr Elgar.

'Mr Robinson,' said Mr Elgar, 'what you found on me only accounted for some of the missing articles?'

'That is so,' said Mr Robinson.

'Did I have the chance of disposing of any memo pads or pencils before I was detained?'

'I don't think you had.'

'So,' said Mr Elgar, 'if more pads and pencils were missing than were found on me, someone else must have taken them.'

'That is so,' said Mr Robinson, 'we've been having rather a lot of thefts recently.'

'So,' I said, 'I suppose you instructed your store detective and your assistants to keep a special look out?'

'That is so, your honour.'

'And, if one or more of your regular customers was a thief, he might possibly notice the extra vigilance?'

'That's possible, your honour.'

'Well, isn't it possible,' I asked, 'that, if a thief had taken several pads and several pencils and suddenly realised that he might be being watched, he'd want to unload some or all of them before he was stopped?'

'That is possible,' said Mr Robinson.

'Well, one way of unloading was to put them into somebody else's pocket, wasn't it?'

'That could be done,' said Mr Robinson.

'Was the store fairly crowded on the day in question?'

'Yes, fairly crowded.'

'Well, Mr Robinson,' I said, 'whatever the truth about Mr Elgar may be, there was a thief other than him around, wasn't there?'

'It looks like it,' said Mr Robinson.

'Well, if the thief took fright, he may have off-loaded two memo pads into Mr Elgar's coat.'

'It could be done,' said Mr Robinson.

'And who,' I asked, 'would be more skilful at doing that than a persistent thief?'

'Oh, they're not pickpockets, your honour,' said Mr Robinson. 'They're shoplifters, which is rather different.'

'There's nothing to prevent a man carrying on both professions, is there?' I asked.

'I suppose not,' said Mr Robinson.

'When you saw Mr Elgar after he'd been detained,' I asked, 'he told you that the pencils were his, and that he'd bought them at another shop, and that he couldn't account for the memo pads?'

'That's true.'

'Well, if someone else had put the pads into his pocket, he wouldn't have been able to account for them, would he?'

'No, he wouldn't.'

No further questions were asked of the manager, and Mr Benton for the defendants agreed that what Mr Elgar had said about the store detective was correct.

I was then addressed both by Mr Benton and by Mr Elgar and finally I gave judgment. Among other things I said this: 'More memo pads were missing than were found on Mr Elgar. So presumably another person had taken some. Which is the more likely, I ask myself, that a man of unblemished reputation should steal a couple of pads, or that a frightened thief might slip them into Mr Elgar's overcoat pocket? It's to be noted that from the very start Mr Elgar said that he couldn't account for the pads. Whatever the truth of the matter, it is not in my opinion more probable that Mr Elgar stole the pads. So on that aspect of the matter the defendants have not proved their case. As to the two pencils, Mr Elgar says that he bought them elsewhere. There's some corroboration of that, though not very much, as I can't place a great deal of reliance on Mrs Long's evidence. But again, which is more probable? That Mr Elgar had stolen them or bought them a few days previously? Certainly not that he had stolen them. But Mr Benton says that, even if the probability was not proved in the case of each separate item, I must take the two together. Look at the coincidences, he says. Well, it is a coincidence, but coincidences do happen. And in my view in this case it's a perfectly credible coincidence, and quite insufficient to prove the defendants' case. In the result, as it is for the defendants to prove that the plaintiff was guilty to justify their dismissing him, and not for him to prove his innocence, I find in Mr Elgar's favour; and hold that the defendants broke their contract when they dismissed him without notice.'

I accordingly gave judgment for the plaintiff for £50 damages and costs.

So in spite of the findings of two criminal courts that Mr Elgar's guilt had been proved beyond all reasonable doubt, I found that it had not even been proved as a probability. Whether it's desirable that a case should be re-tried in this way as a matter of course, I very much doubt. But there will always be the occasional case where it might be the only way to prevent injustice. We can't always do justice, we can only do our best.

Oddly enough there was a further coincidence. After the case was over, I went home by train. And after I'd settled myself down I saw Mr Benton and Mr Elgar come in. They couldn't see me, but I could hear them. Apparently they'd got on very well together during the case, and were on the best of terms. And this is what I heard: 'I'm terribly interested in truth,' said Mr Benton. 'Now that it's all over and you've won, it can't hurt you to tell me the truth. I'll keep it to myself entirely. I promise. Do tell me, did you take the things?'

'What a ridiculous question,' said Mr Elgar. 'What should I want to take a couple of memo pads and pencils for?'

But I feel pretty confident of one thing. Mr Elgar won't do it again.

CHAPTER SIX

The Hidden Money

The origin of this story, as I subsequently learned, was when Amy and Robert Hull got married. It was a perfect wedding. The sun shone, all their relations and friends were there, and nothing could have been happier for the young couple. As they drove away towards their honeymoon, they considered how lucky they were.

'How sweet everybody's been to us,' said Amy, 'how kind.'

'How right you are,' said Robert. 'And that reminds me. What d'you think my uncle has given me? Five hundred premium bonds!'

'Five hundred!' said Amy. 'Oh, he is good.'

'And each one of those,' said Robert, 'might become five thousand pounds, that's two and a half million. We're rich.'

'We're rich anyway,' said Amy. 'We have each other.'

But although the marriage started so auspiciously, it didn't go on like that for very long. Within six months Amy had gone to see a solicitor. He asked her what she wanted.

'I want a divorce,' said Amy.

'Dear, dear,' said the solicitor, 'you're very young.'

'I'm old enough to have the vote,' said Amy, 'so I'm old enough to have a divorce. Anyway, I'm thirty.'

'Are you really? And your husband?'

'He's ten years older.'

'Have you been to the Marriage Guidance Council?' asked the solicitor.

'Look, Mr Gibson,' said Amy, 'if I go to a dairy I go for milk. If I go to a bootmaker I want shoes. And, if I go to a solicitor, I want a divorce, not a flipping Marriage Guidance Council.'

'Be it so, Mrs Hull,' said Mr Gibson, 'but I think you'd better go to a different solicitor.'

'Don't you do divorces?'

'Not yours, I'm afraid. Good morning.'

'Look here,' said Amy, 'you gave me an appointment, and I want to tell you about my case.'

'Your appointment is over, I'm afraid,' said Mr Gibson. 'There'll be no charge.'

'I thought solicitors had to take your case if it was respectable.'

'Barristers, madam,' said Mr Gibson, 'not solicitors. We are allowed to pick and choose our clients. And you'll forgive me, madam, for not choosing you.'

But Amy soon found another solicitor, and he was prepared to take her case. One of the frequent sources of trouble between husband and wife is money. A husband is too mean, or the wife too extravagant – or so each of them says. More than once in the course of their six months' married life, Amy had suggested to Robert that he should sell the premium bonds.

'We haven't had a bean from them. We get no interest. Look at the things we could buy. I'm sure your uncle wanted to make us happy.'

'He wanted to make me happy,' said Robert. 'He never thought much of you.'

'All right,' said Amy, 'keep your blooming premium bonds. Dream about them. Make two and a half millions out of them. Put them under your pillow. They'll be nearer to you than I shall be in the future.'

'That's the best thing I've heard in years,' said Robert. When the break came, Robert was worried about the premium bonds. He had been told – quite rightly – that the Divorce Court goes into the financial side of the parties, both of whom have to declare exactly what they've got, and the amount the husband has to pay to the wife partly depends on what his assets are. As long as Robert had the premium bonds he would have to declare them as part of his assets. He could not bear the thought of Amy having any part of them, so there was only one thing to do, sell them and hide the money. But how? Selling them was easy, but how was he to hide the proceeds? He would be asked what he'd done with the money. How would he successfully pretend to have spent it, but keep it just the same?

That was the origin of the case which I had to try. The action was between Robert Hull and a man called Sandy Morton, and Robert sued to recover from him £500. Robert told me in evidence that he met Mr Morton in a public house, and that he confided to him his trouble about the difficulty of getting rid of the bonds without having to account for the proceeds.

'If I say I've just lost the money, no one will believe me. As far as I can see, I might just as well keep the beastly bonds.'

'I've got an idea,' said Sandy. Robert asked what it was.

'Well I have a share in a club, a gambling club.'

'Well?' asked Robert.

'Suppose you join that club? I take it half a guinea a year won't break you?'

Robert said he could manage that amount, and asked what happened when he joined.

'Well,' said Sandy, 'when you've joined, you gamble.'

'And where does that get me?' asked Robert.

'You gamble away all your five hundred pounds.'

'D'you think I hadn't thought of that?' said Robert 'But just to say you lost the money on a horse or the like is the oldest one in the world. If someone wants to account for the proceeds of a burglary, he says he won it on a horse. If he wants to account for not having money, he says he lost it on a horse. No one believes either of them.'

'And quite rightly,' said Sandy. 'As you say, he didn't win the money on a horse, it was the proceeds of a bank robbery. How can he prove he won it on a horse if he didn't? He can't. And the same applies to losing the money. Two or three pounds, yes. But five hundred? What's the name of the horse or horses? What's the name of the bookmaker? And so on and so forth. You'd soon be broken down over that.'

'I thought that was your solution,' said Robert.

'You thought too soon,' said Sandy. 'Didn't I tell you I was a partner in this club?'

'Yes.'

'Well then,' said Sandy, 'if you lose your money with us, you'll be able to prove it. We'll have chapter and verse for every penny. Now here's an example. We play a game called whisky cribbage. Never mind how it's played, but it needs a bank. Say you take the bank for £100, that's written down in a book. And when that particular bank is finished, either because you're cleaned out or you want to sell it, that's written down too.'

Robert said that he was beginning to understand, and asked Sandy to go on.

'When your case comes up,' said Sandy, 'you'll say you gambled away the money with us, and our records will prove it. We're very particular about records in our business. Just in case someone tries to pull a fast one. Everything is written down and signed for or initialled. No one can say he's put £100 in the game if he's initialled £50. No one can say he's only been paid £50 if he's signed for £100.'

'So,' said Robert, 'you'll be able to show in your records that I've lost £500?'

'On balance,' said Sandy. 'You'll win sometimes, or it would look funny. In fact you'll win at first. Your £500 will swell to, say, £600.'

'That's a marvellous idea,' said Robert. 'When can we begin?'

'Well,' said Sandy, 'I'll introduce you to the club tonight and you'll be a member in a couple of days. Then you must come to the club on the days we put down, so that the doorman and the barman and so on can identify you as having been a regular customer. You'd better have the odd genuine game or two as well so that people can see you playing.'

'I don't mind losing a few pounds,' said Robert.

'You might even win,' said Sandy. 'And then, when the club's closed, we'll make out your story. We'll do it from day to day so that the ink will be all right, and the entries will be in the right place. And at the end of the month we'll have proof positive that you've lost the whole of your £500.'

'Well,' said Robert, 'I'm most grateful to you. But you must have something out of this.'

'Of course,' said Sandy, 'we don't do it for nothing. I'll charge you ten per cent for the service.'

'That's £50?' queried Robert.

'D'you think that's fair?' asked Sandy.

'Very fair,' said Robert. 'When do I pay you?'

'You don't,' said Sandy. 'We'll take it out of the £500.'

'£500?' asked Robert.

'Yes, of course; you must hand that to us. It'll be quite safe in the bank.'

'Is that necessary?' asked Robert.

'Of course it is,' said Sandy. 'Our cash has got to balance, hasn't it? How can we say you've really lost your £500 unless it's gone into our bank? Some of these lawyers are pretty good sleuths, and they'll employ accountants. If you don't pay the money over, they'll go through all the accounts, and at the end they'll say that you haven't paid over one penny piece. "These are just book entries," they'll say.'

Robert said a little doubtfully that he understood.

'But, if you're worried about your money,' went on Sandy, 'I'll show you our bank account. There's plenty there, I assure you. We don't want the £500.'

'So,' said Robert, 'I hand you over £500, and when the case is over, you give me back £450?'

'That's it,' said Sandy. 'But if you don't trust us – '

'Well, I've only known you for a week or so,' said Robert.

'How true,' said Sandy. 'Forget the whole thing.'

'I didn't mean to be offensive, old man,' said Robert.

'Offensive?' said Sandy, 'Of course you're not. I'd feel the same in your case. I wouldn't want to hand over £500 to a comparative stranger without knowing a bit more about him.'

'Well, it's nice of you to put it that way,' said Robert.

'There's no other way to put it. Have another drink.'

Robert went on to tell me that they had one or two drinks, and that then Sandy invited him to come down and see the club, and they went there that evening. At the club they had some more drinks, and eventually Sandy introduced Robert to his partner who was known as Mac. Sandy informed Mac of Robert's problem, and it was not long before Robert changed his mind and decided to leave his £500 with Sandy and Mac.

Robert informed me that Mac seemed a very genuine person, and agreed to do the job for five per cent instead of ten per cent. Mac said that the work involved was trifling, and that £25 was quite enough.

So, according to Robert, they arranged for him to come to the club quite often. He said he deposited the whole of his £500 in cash with Sandy and Mac and after that he did exactly as he was told by them. By the time a month had gone by, there were in addition to the records of the club at least half a dozen witnesses who could testify to the losses made by Robert.

In due course Amy made her claim for alimony, and the solicitors on both sides went into the matter and prepared to fight about it. Robert supplied his solicitors with all the information to show that he'd lost the £500 gambling. And undoubtedly, if Amy's claim for alimony had been heard, Robert would have had a very substantial body of evidence to show that he no longer had the money, and that he had in fact lost it gambling.

But before the application was heard, Amy had second thoughts. It was not long before overtures were made by her to Robert for a reconciliation. And eventually the parties came together again.

As soon as they were living together again, Robert told Amy that he thought it would be a good thing to sell the premium bonds after all, and she was delighted. He admitted to me that he didn't tell her that he'd already sold them and hidden the money. All he had to do now was to collect the money from Sandy and Mac and try and make a more successful second start to his marriage.

So the day after the reconciliation Robert called on Sandy and Mac to get his money. And according to Robert, this is what happened: 'Hello, Mr Hull,' said Sandy, 'haven't seen you for a day or two.'

'I've got some good news,' said Robert, 'my wife and I have made it up again. We're living together.'

'Now isn't that fine?' said Sandy. 'This calls for a celebration. Let's go and find Mac.'

So they found Mac and they went into his private room. Sandy told him what had happened.

'Congratulations, Mr Hull,' said Mac, 'I'm delighted, I really am. There's no better state than that of a happily married man. What'll you have? This is on the house.'

'That's very good of you,' said Robert. 'I ought to be in the chair really.'

'I wouldn't hear of it,' said Mac. 'Tell the barman to open a bottle of champagne, Sandy. I can't tell you how pleased I am. There are too many divorces in this country. The home is the backbone of England.'

Robert said that they then had some drinks and it was suggested that perhaps one day he'd like to bring Amy down to the club, unless she disapproved of gambling on principle.

'I think she'd love it,' said Robert. 'I really am grateful to the two of you. I can't think why you're so good to me.'

'Good to you,' said Mac, 'it's nothing. You're a good customer. We treat all our good customers the same.'

'But I haven't brought you in much,' said Robert.

'Not much? Did you hear him, Sandy? He says he hasn't brought us in much.'

'He's a rich man maybe,' said Sandy, 'and it isn't much to him.'

'Well,' said Robert, 'the profit on the drinks I've had can't be more than a few shillings. I've worked out about even on the genuine bets, so all you'll have had will have been my £25.'

'What's that you said?' said Sandy.

'£25,' repeated Robert.

'£25! You must be dreaming. If you haven't lost £500 in the last month, I'm a Dutchman.'

'Was it as much as that?' said Mac.

'Not much less,' said Sandy.

'I must say you did it very well,' said Robert.

'Did what well?' asked Mac.

'Arranged for me to lose £500.'

'Now you're not saying it wasn't on the level,' said Mac.

'Of course not. All the genuine bets were on the level.'

'And what, pray, were the non-genuine bets?'

'It's all over, I tell you,' said Robert. 'I don't need it any more. I'd like the £500 back, less of course your £25.'

'You'd like it back?' said Sandy.

'Yes, please.'

'The £500 you lost? You'd like it back?'

'Of course.'

'And where would we be,' said Mac, 'if we gave all our losers their money back?'

'But I wasn't a loser,' said Robert. 'Not a real one.' Mac told Sandy to get the records.

'Oh, I know I signed or initialled everything,' said Robert, 'but that was all part of the game.'

'Game,' repeated Sandy, 'what game?'

'What game?' said Mac.

'Look, friends,' said Robert, 'it's been a good joke while it lasted, but it's over now, and I'd like my money back.'

'Well, I'll be damned,' said Mac. 'Drinks my good drink and sits back calmly saying he'd like his money back.'

'Next he'll be saying he's never been here before,' said Sandy.

'Never sat at the tables,' said Mac. 'He'll dispute his signature, that's what he'll do. He'll call us forgers. There's gratitude.'

'I'm tired of this,' said Robert. 'Give me a cheque for £475 and I'll go.'

'Are you asking me or Sandy?' said Mac.

'Both of you. Either of you. I don't care which, I want my money.'

'So do we all want our money,' said Mac. 'And sometimes we want other people's, but we can't have it.'

'It's my money,' said Robert. 'I left it with you so that I could pretend I hadn't got it, and you promised to give it back to me whenever I wanted it.'

'The drink's gone to his head,' said Sandy.

'I hope it's that,' said Mac. 'If it isn't, he seems to be trying to say that we've got his money. And I don't like that sort of talk. Either way, you'd better be going, Mr Hull. If you're drunk, we don't allow that sort of thing on the premises. And if you're just being insulting, we won't have that either.'

'All right,' said Robert. 'I'll go, but I'll sue you.'

'Sue away,' said Mac. 'How many witnesses will you have on your side?'

'I fancy, Mr Hull,' said Sandy, 'that you'll find a good number of people who will be prepared to swear you lost the money gambling.'

'You're a lot of thieves,' said Robert, and left.

He went straight to a solicitor, and in the result the case came in front of me.

After Robert had told me his story, Sandy and Mac gave me their version. They assured me that Robert was simply a gambler who lost his money and was trying to get it back again.

'Your honour,' said Sandy, 'I met him in the pub as he said, but he didn't mention wanting to hide the money. I talked to him about our club, and he said he was interested. So I invited him along. And he lost the money, and that's all there is to it.'

Sandy was then cross-examined by Robert's counsel.

'Mr Sandy Morton,' he was asked, 'you say that the money was simply lost in gambling?'

'I do indeed,' said Sandy.

'Let's see,' said counsel. 'You have, have you not, complete documentary evidence to show every single pound, if not every single penny, that my client lost?'

'That is so, sir,' said Sandy, 'and it's signed or initialled by the plaintiff himself, Mr Robert Hull.'

'Quite so,' said counsel. 'Now tell me, how many regular members of your club are there?'

'Around two or three hundred, I should say.'

'They are people who play regularly?'

'Certainly.'

'Mr Morton,' said counsel, 'for how many of these regular two or three hundred paying members have you such meticulous documentary evidence to show their losses?'

'Some of them win,' said Sandy.

'I dare say,' said counsel, 'but for how many of those who lose have you such complete records as you have in the case of my client?'

'Oh – several.'

'Several! Two or three, d'you mean?'

'More than that,' said Sandy.

'Five or six?'

There was a pause, and Sandy did not answer.

'Mr Morton,' went on counsel, 'if necessary, his honour will order the production of all your books and documents. Are you prepared to swear that you have detailed documentary evidence of the losses of more than half a dozen members in addition to my client?'

'No,' said Sandy, 'I wouldn't swear that.'

'Then,' said counsel, 'why take so much trouble over my client's accounts and these half dozen as well, unless you were just hiding the money for them, and the gaming was a cover?'

'He was a new member,' said Sandy.

'Have you taken the same precautions in the case of each new member?'

'He had no references.'

'Did you ask for any?'

'I can't say that we did.'

'Have you taken the same precautions in the case of each new member who has no references?'

'I can't say that we have.'

'Well, why not?' asked counsel.

There was no answer.

'Why not?' repeated counsel.

'I can't really give a reason,' said Sandy.

'Isn't the reason,' said counsel, 'that there was no real gambling by my client, and you were just keeping the money out of the sight of my client's wife, and his legal advisers?'

'No, sir,' said Sandy, 'and I've witnesses to prove it.'

And Sandy called his witnesses, eight of them altogether, including his partner Mac, the barman, the doorman, and several members of the club. The number of the witnesses was impressive, but the quality of the evidence was less so. When all the evidence was over, I said to counsel for the plaintiff: 'Mr Grove, in one of your questions to Mr Morton, you asked him if the whole object of the exercise wasn't to keep the money out of the sight of Mrs Hull and her legal advisers. That's right, isn't it?'

'Yes, your honour.'

'You might have added to Mrs Hull and her legal advisers, the Divorce Court, mightn't you?'

'What does your honour mean?' asked counsel.

'The object of the exercise,' I said, 'if your client was right, was to keep this £500 from the sights of the Divorce Court, so that any order for alimony or maintenance that might be made would not take into account this £500. Your client wanted that Court to believe that he no longer had the £500.'

'I suppose that's right, your honour,' said counsel.

'In other words,' I said, 'he wanted to deceive the Divorce Court into thinking he had £500 less than in fact he had.'

'Deceive is rather a strong word, your honour,' said counsel.

'You tell me a more appropriate one,' I said. But counsel did not reply.

'Well,' I went on, 'what would you suggest I substitute for "deceive"? This is the truth, isn't it? Your client wanted not only to deceive his wife, but the court to which his wife went as well.'

'I can't really dispute that, your honour.'

'Well,' I said, 'if it's right, how can your client recover money which he handed to the defendant in pursuance of a conspiracy to deceive the Divorce Court?'

'It would be outrageous,' said counsel, 'if the defendant were allowed to keep the money, if my client's story is right.'

'I rather agree,' I said, 'but will this court help your client to recover money which he deposited for the express purpose of deceiving another court? Surely it would be against public policy.'

'But will it not be equally against public policy,' argued counsel, 'for the defendant, who is just as much to blame, to keep this money? It's barefaced robbery.'

'I can't pretend,' I said, 'that, if what your client says is true, I have any sympathy with the defendant. But you know the maxim *in pari delicto*. Where the parties are equally at fault, the defendant wins.'

'Your honour, the defendant hasn't taken this point,' said counsel.

'I know,' I said, 'but I have a duty to take it. If you want time to consider the matter, I'll grant you an adjournment.'

So I granted an adjournment, but before I did so, I said: 'I should like to make it plain to the parties that subject to anything they may say, if I decide this case against the plaintiff on the ground I've mentioned, I shall make no order for costs. If the plaintiff's story is the true one, he certainly doesn't deserve to win his case. The man who goes in for trickery of that kind doesn't deserve to receive any help from any court. But, although for that reason the defendant may win, he also deserves to receive no assistance from the court, and he won't get his costs of defending the case.'

So the case was adjourned. It never came back to me to finish. The plaintiff withdrew his claim and each side paid its own costs. I must say that I should have liked to have been able to order that the money should be forfeited to the state. But that was not possible.

I can't pretend that I liked the idea of the defendant being allowed to keep the money, but I had no sympathy for the plaintiff, who no doubt learned that who sups with the devil must have a long spoon, and that his wasn't long enough.

CHAPTER SEVEN

The Truth

Although in most cases the truth does emerge, however difficult it may at one time seem to arrive at it, there are some cases where it is practically impossible to be certain that one has arrived at it. In the case which forms the subject matter of this story, it appeared at one time that each party, telling an absolutely contradictory account of what had happened, must be telling the truth. And yet one was not. But which?

Mrs Laverton sued Mr Buckland for £300. And this is what she swore had happened. She said that she was sitting in a public house when a man got into conversation with her. She chatted to him for some little time about nothing in particular, and then he asked her why she'd been looking at the advertisements in the paper.

'Are you looking for a job?'

'No. As a matter of fact I'm looking for a house.'

The man, who turned out to be Mr Buckland, the defendant, then said that it was a great piece of luck they had met.

'Are you an estate agent?' asked Mrs Laverton. 'I suppose you are, and that's why you're not easily snubbed.'

But Mr Buckland said that he was not an estate agent, and he added that he was not easily snubbed either.

'I'm in pepper, as a matter of fact,' he said.

'Pepper!' exclaimed Mrs Laverton.

'Now don't say I don't look like a pepper merchant,' said Mr Buckland. 'You've never seen one before.'

'How can a pepper merchant help me with a house?'

Mr Buckland said that that was a very fair question and that the reason he could help was because he'd got a friend who was an estate agent. He then asked her what sort of a house she was looking for. She explained that she was looking for a rooming house as an investment. Mr Buckland asked her how much capital she had, and she explained that she only had £300.

'£300,' repeated Mr Buckland. 'That isn't much, but let me think. If we could find something for about £5,000. Let me see. Eight letting rooms should bring in thirty-five quid a week. Deposit £500, £4,500 on mortgage. Repayment over fifteen years. Say £50 a month. Dead easy. You find £300, I find £200.'

Mrs Laverton said she was a little taken aback at the speed shown by Mr Buckland.

'You're going a bit fast,' she said. 'Who said you were in it?'

'I shouldn't mind as a sideline,' said Mr Buckland, 'but not if you can manage by yourself.'

'Are those figures you mentioned right?' asked Mrs Laverton.

'More or less,' said Mr Buckland.

Mrs Laverton thought for a bit. She knew that £300 was very little. And, if the man would genuinely bring in another £200, it might make it much easier for her to find her investment. Rather hesitantly she agreed to go into the matter further. She said that she gave Mr Buckland her telephone number, and it was arranged that he should ring her when he'd spoken to his friend the estate agent. A few days later he did ring and said that the estate agent had got a house for them, and he suggested that they should see it at once. Mrs Laverton went to meet them, and was introduced by Mr Buckland to the estate agent, Mr Winchcombe.

'Pleased to meet you,' said Mr Winchcombe. 'I'm afraid I shan't be able to come with you to the house. I'm wanted at the office. But I've given the key to Mr Buckland. It's only a few minutes' walk.'

'Do you think it's what I want?' asked Mrs Laverton.

'Quite honestly, madam,' said Mr Winchcombe, 'and to be perfectly frank about it, I think you will be quite delighted. And it's dirt cheap.'

'You've seen it yourself, then?' asked Mrs Laverton.

'I won't make any false pretences, madam,' said Mr Winchcombe. 'No, I haven't. But quite frankly and honestly, I don't think you'll be disappointed. It was a nursing home you wanted it for?'

'No,' said Mrs Laverton, 'it wasn't, as a matter of fact.'

'Oh no, of course,' said Mr Winchcombe, 'that was Mrs Laverton.'

'I *am* Mrs Laverton.'

'Stupid of me, I know,' said Mr Winchcombe. 'Six children and a lot of dogs.'

'No children or dogs,' said Mrs Laverton.

'Dear me,' said Mr Winchcombe, 'I must be slipping. Now you tell me, Mrs Laverton.'

'I want it for a rooming house,' said Mrs Laverton.

'Of course,' said Mr Winchcombe. 'Well, quite frankly and honestly when I saw this house I said to myself – '

But Mrs Laverton interrupted.

'You haven't seen it,' she said.

Mr Winchcombe corrected himself: 'I mean,' he said, 'when my principal told me about it, I said to myself, I said "this is the place for Mrs Leonard"'.

'Laverton,' said Mrs Laverton.

'There I go again,' said Mr Winchcombe. 'Now I mustn't stand gossiping any more, or my principal will think I'm not earning my keep. Go and see it and let us know. Goodbye, Tony boy. Goodbye, Mrs er, Mrs er.' And Mr Winchcombe left, still repeating 'Mrs er.'

Mrs Laverton said that she and Mr Buckland then went to Golders Green to see the house. When they arrived, Mr Buckland said that they were asking £6,500 but he felt sure that they would come down. Mrs Laverton said that she told Mr Buckland that it would fall down before they came down if immediate repairs weren't done to it.

'It is a bit on the dilapidated side,' conceded Mr Buckland.

'A bit,' said Mrs Laverton. 'It would want thousands of pounds spending on it. I'm not even going in.'

Mrs Laverton said that Mr Buckland agreed and invited her out to lunch. A few days later he rang her again, and said on this occasion that he really did think they'd got the house they wanted.

'They want £6,000,' he said, 'and I don't think they'll come down. But if I supply the other hundred, that gives us £600 deposit, and I'm sure we'll get the £5,400 mortgage easily.'

'What about the repayments?' asked Mrs Laverton.

'Easy,' said Mr Buckland. 'Look, £5,400 for fifteen years will work out about £70 a month. Rates another £15. That's £85. Nine letting rooms at £4 a time. That's £36 a week. Simple.'

Mrs Laverton said that they then went to see the house, that she liked it, and it was left that Mr Buckland should try and arrange the financial side of the transaction.

She said that a little later he telephoned and said that everything was arranged, and asked if he could come round and collect.

'Collect?'

'Your £300,' said Mr Buckland. 'You've got it, I suppose?'

'Of course I've got it,' said Mrs Laverton. 'But why this time of night?'

'I want it first thing in the morning,' said Mr Buckland.

'Couldn't I give it to you then?'

'You could,' said Mr Buckland, 'but it would be better tonight. I don't want there to be a slip-up.'

Mrs Laverton explained that, although she felt a little suspicious about the matter, she was very keen on the transaction, and in view of the fact that she'd seen the house, she didn't quite see how anything could go wrong. So she told Mr Buckland that he could come round that evening to collect the money. But she added that he must be quiet when he arrived because she had rather a difficult landlord, who didn't like late visitors.

'I suggest that you whistle "Annie Laurie" when you come to the house, and I'll come down and let you in.'

So in due course Mr Buckland arrived, said Mrs Laverton, and she let him in. Unfortunately they made rather a noise going up the stairs, as Mr Buckland stumbled. Mrs Laverton said that she took him into her room and gave him her £300. He counted it out and then gave her a very strange receipt. According to Mrs Laverton, this is what it said: 'I hereby declare that I, Anthony Buckland, a married man, have this day received from Mrs Laverton the sum of £300 towards the joint purchase of a house. Signed, Anthony Buckland.'

Mrs Laverton said she asked Mr Buckland why he put in about being a married man, to which Mr Buckland replied that, as he was a married man, there seemed no objection to his saying so.

Mrs Laverton said that shortly afterwards her landlord arrived and asked to speak to her. She went and spoke to him for a few minutes, and then came back to her room. A minute or two later, she said, Mr Buckland left. After he'd left, she looked for the receipt which had been left on the table under a book, and could find it nowhere.

The first thing next morning she telephoned to Mr Buckland, but could not get in touch with him. She continued to do this for some days, and eventually called at his house. There she met Mrs Buckland, who showed her the door pretty quickly. She was now, she said, getting very anxious indeed. She had neither her £300, nor the receipt. She wrote to Mr Buckland about it, but received no reply. After this had gone on for a week, she went to the Citizens' Advice Bureau, who suggested that she should go to a solicitor, and this she did.

The solicitor immediately took up the matter with Mr Buckland by writing to him, and asking for the £300 back, and an explanation of his behaviour. After about a week he received a reply saying that Mr Buckland denied the whole transaction. He said that he did not owe Mrs Laverton a penny, that he'd never had £300 from her, and he'd never given her a receipt for it, and that he didn't understand what she was talking about. In consequence of this, the solicitor issued a summons, and this was duly served upon Mr Buckland,

But, although Mr Buckland had denied owing the money, he did not put in a defence to the summons within the time limited by the rules, and in due course Mrs Laverton's solicitor obtained judgment against him for

£300 and costs. But, as the money wasn't paid, Mrs Laverton's solicitor put in execution on Mr Buckland's goods, at the house where he lived. There was an immediate reaction from Mr Buckland. He applied to have the judgment set aside on the ground that he had gone abroad and forgotten about it, and that in fact he didn't owe the money.

The application came in front of me, and I asked Mr Buckland's solicitor whether, in order to demonstrate his good faith in the matter, Mr Buckland was prepared to bring the whole of the £300 into court to abide the result of the trial. Mr Buckland, through his solicitor, unhesitatingly agreed. Accordingly, as soon as the £300 had been paid into court, I set aside the judgment, and ordered that the action should be tried. I had already ordered Mr Buckland to pay any costs that had been thrown away by his failure to put in a defence in time, and it was obviously just that, if he brought the money into court, he should have an opportunity of putting forward his defence in full.

So eventually the case came on before me for trial. And Mrs Laverton told to me the story which I have already related. But, before I tell you what Mr Buckland said, I ought to tell you something which happened before he gave his evidence.

When the case was called on, counsel for the defendant, Mr Buckland, got up and made an application to me.

'Your honour,' he said, 'when I came into court this morning, I noticed my friend was looking at some documents. I asked him if they were anything to do with the case, and he said that they were. I then asked him if they were privileged from production, and he said that they weren't. So I asked if I could see them. To my surprise he said I couldn't. I asked why not. He said because he wouldn't show them to me. I said I should apply to your honour. He said that was up to me. So here I am applying to your honour to order my friend to show me the documents.'

'Has there been discovery in the case?' I asked.

Perhaps I should explain that 'discovery' is a technical legal term, and is the means by which each party, if ordered to do so, has to show the other side all the documents in his possession which are not privileged from production and are material to the case. In the county court there is often no formal order for discovery, and the parties just show each other the documents which they are relying upon.

'No, your honour,' said counsel. 'There's been no order for discovery, but the parties have written to each other disclosing various documents, but plainly not those which my friend was looking at.'

So I asked counsel for the plaintiff why he wouldn't show the documents.

'Because,' he said, 'in my opinion it would not be in the interests of justice to do so.'

Now I knew that this was one of those cases where there were very good reasons for believing both parties, and yet one was lying. And knowing the difficulty of arriving at the truth in such cases, I must admit that I was ready to welcome anything which would show where the truth lay. The plaintiff's counsel said that it was not in the interests of justice to show the documents at that stage. And I decided to leave things as they were.

'As there's been no actual order for discovery,' I said, 'and there is no application for an adjournment in order to obtain one, I shall say nothing further in the matter. Let the case proceed.'

Before Mr Buckland gave his evidence, Mrs Laverton was of course cross-examined by Mr Buckland's counsel about her story. Among other things she was asked these questions: 'Mrs Laverton,' asked counsel, 'you say that this £300 was the whole of your savings.'

'Yes.'

'Out of what had you saved them?'

'Out of my earnings. I worked in a shop for three years.'

'And where did you keep them?'

'At home.'

'Rather dangerous, wasn't it,' asked counsel, 'to keep such a large sum at home?'

'I suppose so, but I liked the idea of having it by me when the time came.'

'Have you never heard of the Post Office Savings Bank?'

'Yes.'

'Why not put the money into that? It's much safer, and you'd get a little interest.'

'Perhaps I should have, but I didn't.'

'Had you, by any chance, a Post Office Savings account, Mrs Laverton?' asked counsel.

'As a matter of fact, I had,' said Mrs Laverton. 'I have the book here.'

The book showed that she'd never had more than £50 in the account.

'Why on earth,' said counsel, 'didn't you put this £300 into the Post Office too?'

'It may have been silly,' said Mrs Laverton, 'not to. But I liked the idea of this money, which I was saving for the express purpose of buying a house, being with me all the time.'

'One burglar,' I said, 'and you might have lost it all.'

'I have lost it all,' said Mrs Laverton.

'But not through a burglar,' I said.

'As good as,' said Mrs Laverton.

'Not really, madam,' I said. 'You handed this money, so you say, quite willingly to Mr Buckland. A burglar would have taken it against your will.'

'I've lost it just the same,' said Mrs Laverton.

'No doubt,' I said, 'but at the moment I don't quite understand why you were careful with your £50 and put it in the Post Office, but took the risk of losing a sum very much larger.'

'I can't give any other explanation,' said Mrs Laverton. 'I wanted to have the money by me.'

'Mr Buckland,' went on counsel, 'says that you never had £300 to hand to him.'

'How can he know what I had?' said Mrs Laverton.

'Well, he says you never handed him £300 or any sum.'

'He's a liar.'

'So you say. He also says that you became lovers.'

'That's another lie,' said Mrs Laverton.

'Are you sure of that?' asked counsel.

'Certainly.'

'You're a woman of exemplary character?'

'I wouldn't say that,' said Mrs Laverton. 'Who is? But I've never been in any sort of trouble.'

'That's what I mean,' said counsel. 'And no doubt in due course my learned friend is going to say to his honour: "Why should a respectable woman make a false claim for £300?" May I suggest to you the reason?'

'You may suggest what you like,' said Mrs Laverton, 'but he's had my £300.'

'I suggest to you,' said counsel, 'that you've done this to punish Mr Buckland for breaking off his relationship with you.'

'Rubbish,' said Mrs Laverton. 'There never was any relationship.'

'Would you agree,' went on counsel, 'that in history, in plays and novels, in the ordinary course of life, a woman scorned will do things which she'd never normally dream of doing?'

'I am not a woman scorned,' said Mrs Laverton.

'But you've heard of such women?'

'I suppose so.'

'Sometimes they've committed murder.'

'I may have read something of the sort,' said Mrs Laverton.

'Murder,' went on counsel, 'because their lovers left them.'

'What's that to do with me?' said Mrs Laverton.

'Sometimes,' said counsel, 'they write scurrilous letters.'

'Perhaps they do,' said Mrs Laverton.

'Or assault the man in the street.'

'What *has* this to do with me?' said Mrs Laverton,

'This,' said Mr Buckland's counsel, 'this, Mrs Laverton. I suggest that on this occasion you have sued for £300 which you know perfectly well is not due to you.'

'That is absolutely untrue,' said Mrs Laverton.

'Can you suggest any reason,' went on counsel, 'why a perfectly respectable man like my client should take £300 off you and pretend he hasn't?'

'He wouldn't be the first person to do a thing like that,' said Mrs Laverton. 'I told him I'd got £300, and he decided to get it out of me, and he has.'

'Tell me another thing,' said counsel. 'You said that he made out a receipt, put it on the table, and covered it with a book. If your landlord hadn't asked you to come out of the room, he wouldn't have had a chance of taking it from you, would he?'

'He'd have found some other way, I expect,' said Mrs Laverton.

'But how?' persisted counsel,

'Don't ask me,' said Mrs Laverton; 'sleight of hand, anything. A man who's behaved as he has would know a thing or two.'

'You don't seem to like him,' said counsel.

'Would you like a man who'd lifted £300 off you?'

'When you came back from your landlord, was the receipt still on the table?'

'I've no idea.'

'But surely you'd have noticed.'

'Well, I didn't.'

'You'd just parted with your life savings, surely you'd want to make certain that you had the receipt.'

'I didn't think of it till too late. It was only after Mr Buckland had left that I wanted to put the receipt away in a safe place, and then I couldn't find it.'

'You wanted to put the receipt in a safe place?' queried counsel.

'Of course.'

'Because,' went on counsel, 'it was the only record you had of your £300?'

'Yes.'

'And you thought it very important to preserve it. It was really worth £300?'

'Certainly.'

'And you'd hate to lose £300?'

'Of course.'

'Well,' said counsel, 'if you were so keen on keeping the receipt safely, why didn't you keep the £300 safely – in the Post Office?'

'I kept the £300 safely enough until Mr Buckland came along,' said Mrs Laverton.

'That was the last time you saw him till you saw him again in court?'

'Yes.'

'So it's only after he's shown that he doesn't want any more of your company that you claim he's had £300 off you?'

I then intervened and said that counsel had made his points clearly enough.

'You say,' I said, 'that this action is brought out of spite, and it's odd that a woman with a Post Office Savings account should keep £300 loose in the house?'

'It wasn't loose, your honour,' said Mrs Laverton, 'I kept it all together.'

'Quite so,' I said.

I was now beginning to see a little daylight. Although it was unusual for a woman of good character to bring a case like this if it had no foundation, if there *had* been an affair between these two people, it could account for anything. But, of course, I must first see what sort of a witness Mr Buckland was. His story followed the line taken by his counsel in cross-examination of Mrs Laverton. And he told it well enough. He was then cross-examined by Mrs Laverton's counsel.

'Mr Buckland,' was the first question, 'you've taken an oath to tell the truth in this case.'

'I have.'

'How much importance do you attach to the oath?'

'How d'you mean?'

'How much importance d'you attach to the oath?' repeated counsel.

'As much as you do, I suppose.'

'Counsel doesn't take an oath or give evidence, we just ask questions. Would you break your oath?'

'Certainly not.'

'Have you never broken an oath?'

'I've never given evidence before.'

'I didn't ask you that. I asked if you'd never broken an oath?'

'What d'you mean by an oath?' asked Mr Buckland.

'I mean whatever you mean. Have you never broken what you consider to be an oath?'

'You're thinking about my affair with Mrs Laverton, I suppose,' said Mr Buckland, 'and my marriage vows.'

'Have you ever broken what you consider to be an oath?' repeated counsel.

'In that respect, yes. And I won't be the first or the last man to do it. Or woman either.'

'You're not suggesting,' said counsel, 'that my client was a married woman?'

'She said,' said Mr Buckland, 'that she was a widow, but for all I know she may have a husband somewhere.'

'Would it satisfy you if I produced Mr Laverton's death certificate?'

'I don't care what you produce,' said Mr Buckland. 'All I say is that I broke my marriage vows. But I didn't steal her £300.'

'Your case is,' said counsel, 'that you broke off the affair because she started to get money out of you.'

'Yes, like she's trying to do now. She did it very delicately, I grant you. One night when I went round to have a bit of fun she said she wasn't in the mood. I asked what was up, and she said that her brother owed £20 and couldn't pay. So of course I gave it to her, and lo and behold! she was in the mood. Well, I didn't mind that. She's a good-looking woman. £20 was a fair price.'

'How dare you!' screamed Mrs Laverton from the middle of the court.

'If you're in the right, Mrs Laverton,' I said, 'I can quite understand your anger. But you must please control yourself and not interrupt the proceedings.'

'Then a week later,' went on Mr Buckland, 'she wasn't in the mood again. This time it was her sister, and £30. Well, I could see what was coming, so I just beat it. And that's all there is to the whole case.'

'Have you ever discussed buying houses with her?' asked counsel.

'The only mention of houses,' said Mr Buckland, 'was when she told me when I first met her that she'd like to get a house but hadn't any money. And I said, if you haven't any money, you can't buy a house.'

'You never went to see a house with her?'

'Certainly not.'

'You never worked out any figures with her?'

'No.'

'You never met Mr Winchcombe with her?'

'Of course I didn't.'

'Never went to a house near Golders Green which was in very bad repair?'

'No.'

'It's all invention, is it, by Mrs Laverton to try and get £300 out of you?'

'Exactly,' said Mr Buckland.

At that stage my mind was working like this. The plaintiff had to prove her case. It was for her to prove that the probability was that she'd been cheated out of her money; it was not for Mr Buckland to prove that he hadn't taken it. So that, if there was nothing to choose between the parties, the plaintiff would fail. But it seemed to me at this stage that, unless Mr Buckland suddenly crumpled up in cross-examination, not only was the balance not falling in Mrs Laverton's favour, but, if anything, it was being tipped against her. It is true that, if Mr Buckland's story was true, he'd broken his marriage vows, but Mrs Laverton wasn't a young girl, and she'd been a willing party to it. So there was nothing to choose between them on that score. But, whereas I could think of no obvious reason for a respectable man – and as far as the evidence went Mr Buckland was quite as respectable as Mrs Laverton – for a respectable man suddenly stealing £300 from a woman, this story of a broken-off affair could certainly account for Mrs Laverton's claim being a false one. And moreover she had no very satisfactory explanation for keeping £300 in cash in her room. People do do that sort of thing, but not often if they have Post Office Savings accounts. So at that stage I said to myself that, if counsel for Mrs Laverton couldn't make any better headway with Mr Buckland, Mrs Laverton was going to lose her case. But then Mrs Laverton's counsel handed a document through the usher to Mr Buckland, and asked him if it was in his handwriting. Mr Buckland admitted that it was.

'Does this document not show a figure of £5,500 on the left-hand side, and figures adding up to £35 on the right?'

'Yes,' said Mr Buckland.

'It looks,' said counsel, 'like the price of a house on the one side, and the rents that could be obtained on the other, doesn't it?'

'She might have taken it out of my pocket one night,' said Mr Buckland.

'So you agree that it was written for the purpose of working out the profits to be made from a rooming house?'

'I suppose it was,' said Mr Buckland.

'Now look at this other document, please.' And counsel handed another document to the usher to be taken to Mr Buckland. 'Is that also in your handwriting?'

'Yes, it is.'

'Does this show the name of a Mrs Price, and her telephone number and – '

At that stage, counsel for Mr Buckland got up and said: 'Your honour, I must protest most vigorously.'

'Yes, what do you want to say?' I asked.

'These must be the documents,' said counsel, 'that my learned friend was looking at this morning and which he refused to show me. If we'd known about them, we might have called other witnesses, Mr Winchcombe, Mrs Price, and I dare say others.'

'Quite so,' I said. 'Do you apply for an adjournment to call these witnesses?'

'I most certainly do, your honour,' said counsel.

'Well of course,' I said, 'you're entitled to an adjournment. And, if your opponent has any objection, I shall overrule it. You say these documents have taken you by surprise, and that you must have an opportunity to deal with them.'

'Exactly, your honour,' said counsel.

I then addressed counsel for Mrs Laverton.

'What d'you say about an adjournment?' I asked.

'I've no objection at all,' said counsel.

'Very well,' I said. 'I shall grant an adjournment to enable the defendant's counsel to call these additional witnesses to corroborate his case. But,' I added to counsel, 'if when the time comes you *don't* call them, I may draw my own conclusions. Just before we adjourn, I'd like to ask Mr Buckland one question. Mr Buckland,' I asked, 'are you suggesting that Mrs Laverton took the second document out of your pocket, too?'

Mr Buckland did not answer.

'Well, Mr Buckland?' I repeated.

Mr Buckland still did not answer.

'I shall assume, then,' I said, 'that you're not. No doubt when the case comes on again you will explain how it is that Mrs Laverton had in her possession documents in your handwriting which seem to show that she is plainly right when she says the purchase of a rooming house was gone into between you and that you are plainly wrong when you deny this.'

So the case was adjourned and I was not surprised when I was told by the clerk that I would not hear any more of it. The parties had settled the matter. And the settlement consisted in Mr Buckland agreeing to pay £250 to Mrs Laverton and an agreed sum for her costs. There is always a risk in litigation and the costs are heavy. And no doubt the plaintiff's advisers were wise to let the plaintiff sacrifice £50 to make sure of victory.

So by the production of those two documents, the course of the case was completely changed. At the time when they were produced I'd entirely forgotten about the original application at the beginning of the case, and I was as much surprised by the documents as was Mr Buckland. But, had Mr Buckland been shown those documents before he gave his evidence, he could easily, had he been so minded, have changed his story slightly to account for them. He could have said, for example, that *he* was interested in buying the house for himself and that he'd talked about it to Mrs Laverton – his girlfriend. No doubt, if he'd remembered that he'd given her the documents, he'd have done so. But he'd forgotten. Now do you remember what counsel for Mrs Laverton said when he refused to produce the documents?

'I don't think it will be in the interests of justice to do so,' he said.

How right he was.

CHAPTER EIGHT

Made to Measure

The registrar of a County Court has two functions. In the first place he is responsible for the entire administration of the court. His other function is mainly to try small cases. From his decision in those cases the litigant has the right of appeal to the judge. There is normally a very good relationship between the judge and the registrar, and I was on the best of terms with the registrar in my court.

One day he came into my room in the middle of the day, when I was just preparing to go home. It had been, from my point of view, one of those lucky occasions when a long case had been settled, and there was nothing else for me to do. So I had arranged to meet my wife and go and look at some pictures.

'Hello, Charles,' I said, 'what can I do for you?'

'You've finished your list, I see,' he said.

'I have.'

'Oh,' he said, and hesitated.

I had a pretty good idea of what was to come.

'Go on,' I said, 'tell me. What is it you want me to do? I was just going to look at some pictures with my wife.'

'Oh, I wouldn't stop you for the world, judge,' he said.

'But that's exactly what you've come to do,' I replied.

'Really,' he said, 'I'd hate to spoil your afternoon.'

133

'Then why come here?' I said.

'Admittedly,' he answered, 'that is a question.'

'Well,' I said, 'out with it. What is it you want me to do? I suppose I'd better put my robes on again?'

'I hate doing this to you,' he said.

'You love it,' I replied. 'You grudge me every idle moment – but of course I'll help if I can.'

'It is good of you,' he said, 'and I'm most grateful. I'm glad you take so long in disrobing. The last judge we had here would have been out and away before I could have got into his room.'

'And the next judge,' I said, 'may refuse to do it anyway. Never mind. What is it? I'm resigned.'

'Tell me, judge,' he said, 'have you ever had a chap called Kiddington in front of you?'

I didn't remember having had such a litigant in front of me, and I said so.

'Well,' said the regi strar, 'I'd be awfully grateful if you'd try a case of his. I've had three in the last couple of months, and have always decided against him. He's really a very nice fellow, but he's a bit odd, and always seems to me to be in the wrong. He never appeals from my decisions, but there is a hurt look on his face when I decide against him that makes me feel as though I were hitting a child.'

'You say he's a bit odd,' I said, 'perhaps it's you who are a bit odd?'

'Exactly,' said the registrar. 'So I just wondered whether perhaps I'm not on his wavelength, and I thought it might be a good idea if you didn't mind, if you tried his next case.'

'What's it about?' I asked.

'A suit,' said the registrar. 'He says it doesn't fit.'

'And won't pay?'

134

'Yes.'

'Have you had the tailor before you in other cases?'

'Yes. He's quite a decent chap too. I think you'll like them both.'

'How long will it take?'

'Well, it really depends on how you get on with Mr Kiddington.'

'Well, if it only takes half an hour,' I said, 'I ought to be able to get away in time to meet my wife.'

'Quite,' said the registrar. But he said it so doubtfully that I realised he hadn't told me all.

'You're keeping something back from me,' I said.

'I'd never do a thing like that,' he answered, 'would I?'

'I'll ring up my wife and tell her I'm not coming. Of course,' I added a little more hopefully, 'they might settle the case.'

'That,' said the registrar very definitely, 'they most certainly will not do. Mr Kiddington does not settle his cases. He comes to the court to get justice. Three times I've sent him away empty-handed.'

'Now, Charles,' I said, 'I'm not going to decide in his favour just to please you.'

'I really am most grateful,' he said, and left me.

So rather reluctantly I put on my robes again and eventually went into court and the case was called on. The plaintiff was a Mr William Jones and he was represented by Mr Benton, whom you will have met in previous stories. The defendant conducted his own case.

After the case had been called on, Mr Benton got up and opened the facts to me.

'May it please your honour,' he said, 'this is a simple little case of a claim for twenty-five guineas by my client, who is a tailor, against the defendant. The only defence is that the suit didn't fit.'

'Was it made to measure?' I asked.

'Yes, your honour,' said Mr Benton. And then he added: 'Your honour, I think Mr Kiddington, the defendant, wants to say something to you.'

'How d'you know?' I asked.

'Well,' said Mr Benton, 'he's moving his hands along the front of the witness box, and that's always a sign that he wants to say something.'

'I see,' I said. 'Are there any other codes going to be used in this case, Mr Benton?'

'I suggest, your honour,' said Mr Benton, 'that you wait and see.'

'Very well,' I said. 'Is it right, Mr Kiddington, that you want to say something?'

'Yes,' said Mr Kiddington, 'very much. I do want to say something. Yes, your honour, please. Counsel is right, I want to say something. I want to say it now. Are you receiving me loud and clear?'

I now realised why the registrar had wanted me to try the case. My view is that, when you get litigants who are perhaps a little bit unusual, you should not call them to order, but as far as possible you should run with them, and help them to explain their side of the case.

'What is it you want to say, Mr Kiddington?'

'Shall I say it from here?' said Mr Kiddington. 'Or may I go into counsel's row?'

'You may speak from where you wish, Mr Kiddington,' I said.

'Your honour is extremely kind.'

'Now,' I said, 'what is it you want to say?'

'No,' said Mr Kiddington.

'No what?' I asked.

'Just no,' said Mr Kiddington.

'But what does it mean?'

'It's the direct negative, your honour. No, not, never.'

'Can you help me, Mr Benton?' I said.

'I suggest,' said Mr Benton, 'that your honour asks him "what is not?"'

'What is not?' I repeated.

'What is not,' said Mr Benton quite firmly.

'Very well then,' I said. 'Mr Kiddington, what is not?'

'Made to measure,' said Mr Kiddington.

'You mean,' I said, 'that the suit was not made to measure?'

'No, not, never,' said Mr Kiddington.

'So that's the dispute, Mr Benton, is it?' I said. 'Was the suit ready-made or made to measure?'

'Not exactly, your honour,' said Mr Benton. 'I think that both sides will agree that my client contracted to make a suit to measure. But Mr Kiddington says that because it didn't fit, it was not made to measure.'

'Is that right, Mr Kiddington?' I asked.

'No, not, never.'

'That means it's right, I take it, Mr Benton?'

'Yes, your honour,' said Mr Benton.

'I think I'm getting the hang of it,' I said. 'So the only question which I have to decide is, did the suit fit? I rather gather Mr Kiddington would like to say something more. He's wiping the desk in front of him.'

'No, your honour,' said Mr Benton, 'when he's standing there, that only means he would like to sit down.'

'Pray sit down, Mr Kiddington,' I said.

'Thank you, your honour,' said Mr Kiddington. 'I'm now sitting where perhaps your honour once sat himself. Or should I say, where your honour once sat yourself? They're rather difficult these phrases. At least I find them so.'

'Shall we get on with the case, Mr Kiddington?' I said.

'That's what I'm here for, your honour. All I want is justice.'

'You won't necessarily get it here, Mr Kiddington,' I said.

'But I thought – ' said Mr Kiddington, and paused.

'You thought you'd come to a court of justice, Mr Kiddington?'

'Precisely.'

'So you have,' I said. 'But it's only a court of human justice, not of absolute justice. We do our best, but we are bound to make mistakes from time to time.'

'Well, your honour,' asked Mr Kiddington, 'are you going to make a mistake this time? It would save us all a lot of trouble if you could tell us in advance and then we could go home.'

As I seemed a little uncertain what to do about Mr Kiddington's last remark, Mr Benton intervened.

'If I might intervene, your honour,' he said. 'I've had considerable experience of being against Mr Kiddington, and I think I can assure your honour that he has no intention of being contemptuous of the court or of your honour, or of anybody else.'

'No, not, never,' corroborated Mr Kiddington.

'Very well then,' I said, 'shall we get on with the case? Mr Benton, perhaps you would like to call Mr Jones.'

So Mr Jones, the plaintiff, duly came into the witness box and took the oath. And then he was asked by Mr Benton about the order for the suit.

'Did the suit fit him when it was finished, Mr Jones?'

'If I do not live to say another word,' said Mr Jones, 'it fitted him better than any other suit that I have made.'

'Thank you, Mr Jones,' said Mr Benton.

I then invited Mr Kiddington to cross-examine. His first question was: 'Mr Jones, have you made many suits in your lifetime?'

'Many thousands.'

'I take it they didn't fit?'

'What are you saying? Of course they fitted.'

'But you've just sworn they didn't.'

'I swore no such thing.'

'D'you say that the suit you made for me was a perfect fit?'

'I do.'

'D'you say that the suits you made for other people were perfect fits?'

'I do.'

'Then how can mine have been a better fit than any suit you'd made before?'

'I do not understand,' said Mr Jones.

'Mr Jones,' I said, 'it's quite true that you did say that if you never said another word, the suit you made for Mr Kiddington was a better fit than any other suit you'd made. And Mr Kiddington now says that if it was a better fit, the other suits were not as good fits, and therefore they didn't fit properly.'

'All the suits I make to order fit properly,' said Mr Jones.

'When I came into your shop,' asked Mr Kiddington, 'did I not ask you if you could guarantee to make a suit exactly as I wanted, and didn't you say that you would?'

'That is quite correct.'

'And when I brought the suit back to you, didn't I say that it was not exactly as I wanted it?'

'You said a lot of things,' said Mr Jones. 'Half of them I couldn't understand. All I did know was that the suit fitted you to perfection. If you try it on now, his honour can see for himself.'

'But what is perfection, Mr Jones?' asked Mr Kiddington.

'Perfection is perfection.'

'But,' said Mr Kiddington, 'what is perfect to one person is not perfect to another. What is perfect to his honour may not be perfect to me. What is perfect to me may not be perfect to his honour. What is perfect to Mr Benton may not be perfect to you. What is perfect to you may not be perfect to Mr Benton. What is perfect to the usher may not be perfect to the clerk. What is perfect to the clerk may not be perfect to the usher. What is perfect to the – '

I then intervened.

'Mr Benton,' I asked, 'what is the code for "this must stop", please?'

'If your honour just leaves it for a moment or two,' said Mr Benton, 'I think it will stop of its own accord.'

'What is perfect for the dancer,' went on Mr Kiddington, 'is not perfect for the typist. What is perfect for the actor is not perfect for the soldier. That's about all, I think, your honour.'

'But is it agreed between you,' I asked, 'that the suit was to be a perfect fit, whatever that may mean?'

'No, not, never,' said Mr Kiddington.

'Then what was it to be, Mr Kiddington?'

'It was to be exactly as I wanted it,' he said.

'D'you agree with that, Mr Jones? Was the suit to be made exactly as Mr Kiddington wanted it?' I asked.

'He said so much,' said Mr Jones, 'I really couldn't say what he did want. But I measured him for the suit, and I made it to his requirements. What more can a man do?'

'You didn't have to take the business, Mr Jones,' said Mr Kiddington.

'If I'd known what it involved, I certainly wouldn't have,' was the reply.

'So far as you could tell, Mr Jones,' asked Mr Benton, 'did you make the suit exactly as Mr Kiddington ordered?'

'Yes.'

'Did I ask you to make one leg rather longer than the other?' asked Mr Kiddington.

'Yes.'

'Did you do so?'

'I did.'

'Then it can't have been a perfect fit, can it?'

'It was what you wanted.'

'But you've sworn it was a perfect fit.'

'It was a perfect fit,' said Mr Jones, 'in accordance with your requirements.'

'Did you put three buttons on one sleeve, and two on the other?'

'I did.'

'Had you any idea why I wanted that?'

'Not the faintest.'

'Well, try and think now.'

'I still haven't the faintest idea.'

'Perhaps your honour will explain,' said Mr Kiddington, 'why I wanted three buttons on one sleeve, and two on the other.'

'I'm afraid I can't,' I said.

'Not even you, your honour? Mr Benton, then.'

'No, Mr Kiddington,' said Mr Benton, 'I'm afraid you have me there too.'

'Well, isn't it obvious, your honour?' said Mr Kiddington. 'I wanted to be reminded of something. If you've got three buttons on each sleeve, it can't remind you of anything except that you have three buttons on each sleeve. But if you've got three buttons on one sleeve, and two buttons on the other, then it can remind you of a great many things.'

'I suppose, Mr Kiddington,' I said, 'that if you have no buttons on your trousers, it will remind you that they may fall down.'

'It wouldn't remind *me*, your honour,' said Mr Kiddington. 'I don't wear braces, you see, never have, they're bad for the shoulders. Anyone can see that Mr Benton does wear braces. It doesn't so much matter now, but in ten or fifteen years' time, he'll be a bent old man like your honour.'

'Mr Kiddington,' I said, 'you really shouldn't talk like that.'

'No, your honour,' said Mr Kiddington, 'I shouldn't talk like that. I really shouldn't. Would your honour be kind enough to tell me if I do it again? It comes of not having two buttons on one sleeve and three on the other. That would have reminded me.'

'Mr Benton,' I said, 'I really would like to know whether you agree that your client had to make a suit exactly in accordance with Mr Kiddington's requirements. And by requirements I don't mean his requirements after the suit was made, but the requirements he stated before the suit was made.'

'Yes,' said Mr Benton, 'I do agree.'

'Then, Mr Jones,' I asked, 'are Mr Kiddington's legs of different size?'

'Everyone's legs are different in size,' said Mr Jones.

'You mean,' I asked, 'that one leg is longer or shorter than the other?'

'Exactly.'

'Then are all the trouser legs that you make for all your customers different in size from each other?'

'No.'

'Why not, if the legs are different in size?'

'Because the difference is so small,' said Mr Jones, 'that we don't take any notice of it in most cases. But the defendant said that in his case there was half an inch in it.'

'Was there?' I asked.

'No,' said Mr Jones.

'But you made the trouser legs in his case half an inch different?'

'Yes, I did.'

'Then they didn't fit properly?'

'No, they didn't.'

'But I thought you said it was a perfect fit,' I said.

'A perfect fit in accordance with his requirements,' said Mr Jones. 'If he asks for two legs with different sizes, well then, I give him two legs with different sizes. He can have what he likes as far as I'm concerned.'

'Did you undertake to make a suit to satisfy me?' said Mr Kiddington.

'I may have done,' said Mr Jones.

'Well, didn't you know at the time,' said Mr Kiddington, 'that I was, what you might call, an awkward customer?'

'No, I certainly didn't.'

'But that's how you would describe me now?'

'I certainly would.'

'And d'you agree, Mr Jones, an awkward customer may require awkward things?'

'Yes,' said Mr Jones, 'I certainly agree to that.'

'Have you ever had any customers as awkward as me before?' asked Mr Kiddington.

'I certainly haven't, and I don't want any in the future either.'

'That wasn't a very kind thing to say, was it?' said Mr Kiddington.

'I haven't come here to be kind,' said Mr Jones, 'I've come here for my money.'

'What other special requirements, if any, did Mr Kiddington make, Mr Jones?' I asked.

'I must look in my book,' said Mr Jones.

He looked in his book and then said: 'He wanted one trouser leg with a turn-up, and one without. He wanted lining on one side of the coat only. The right. No, I mean the left.'

'Well,' said Mr Kiddington, 'which is it?'

'The left.'

'Are you sure it isn't the right?'

'Mr Jones,' I asked, 'when you heard these rather unusual requirements of Mr Kiddington, didn't you think you were dealing with a rather unusual customer?'

'Yes, I suppose I did.'

'Didn't you think it a little dangerous to accept an order from such an unusual customer? After all, if he'd made these very strange requirements, was it not at least possible that when you'd made the suit he would refuse to accept it on some unusual ground?'

'I never thought about it, your honour,' said Mr Jones. 'I make suits to please my customers. If you want one leg ten inches shorter than the other, you can have it as far as I'm concerned.'

'It might remind you not to walk in a puddle,' said Mr Kiddington.

'Well,' I said, 'there's not much point in my seeing the suit on Mr Kiddington until I know exactly what requirements were made by him when he gave the order for the suit.'

'Perhaps Mr Jones would read them out, your honour,' put in Mr Benton.

'Apart from the things I've mentioned, your honour,' said Mr Jones, 'he wanted a circular hole in the back of the waistcoat.'

'That,' said Mr Kiddington, 'was to remind me to sit down, your honour.'

'To sit down.' I asked. 'To sit down when?'

'When I was tired, your honour.'

'And there were to be two pockets in the waistcoat,' went on Mr Jones, 'but they were to be sewn up.'

'Sewn up?' I queried.

'Yes, your honour.'

'You mean,' I said, 'that you actually made the pockets and then sewed them up so that they could be of no use?'

'Exactly, your honour.'

'Mr Kiddington,' I said, 'I suppose that was to remind you not to put your hands in your pockets?'

'My parents advised it, your honour,' said Mr Kiddington, 'or one of them. My father or my mother. At this distance of time it's a little difficult for me to remember. That's one of my complaints against Mr Jones, your honour. If he'd put the button hole in the right place, I should have remembered.'

'But you're not wearing the suit he made for you.'

'Exactly, your honour. If he'd made it properly, I shouldn't have been here.'

'Then,' I said, 'the question of remembering whether it was your father or your mother wouldn't have arisen.'

'Exactly, your honour,' said Mr Kiddington. 'Now you can see why I'm so upset about it all.'

'What is your next question?' I asked.

'Next question to you, your honour, or to the witness?' said Mr Kiddington.

'You're not entitled to ask me questions,' I said.

'No one told me that before I came,' said Mr Kiddington.

'Well, I'm telling you now.'

'Can I have it in writing, your honour?'

'You can not.'

'But they may ask me when I get home.'

'I can't help that.'

'Would you come back with me and explain, your honour?'

'Mr Benton,' I said, 'how long does this go on for?'

'You should ask me that, your honour,' said Mr Kiddington. 'How can he tell?'

'All right,' I said, 'I do ask you, Mr Kiddington, how long will it go on for?'

'Isn't that a matter for you, your honour?' said Mr Kiddington. 'You're in charge of the case, not me.'

'Well, I'm glad to hear it,' I said. 'As I'm in charge of it, I must ask you to go on questioning Mr Jones.'

'That's what I've been waiting to do, your honour,' said Mr Kiddington. 'Now, Mr Jones, why are you suing me? Tell me why.'

'Because I want my money, of course.'

'Why haven't I paid you?' asked Mr Kiddington.

'You should know that,' said Mr Jones.

'You don't think I'd get out of my just liabilities, do you?' asked Mr Kiddington.

'You'd be capable of getting out of anything.'

'That's a very unfriendly thing to say,' said Mr Kiddington, 'do you really mean it?'

'You'd feel unfriendly if someone didn't pay his debts to you,' said Mr Jones.

'I wouldn't if he had a good reason.'

'Well, you haven't a good reason.'

'But I say I have.'

'But I say you haven't.'

'Have.'

'Haven't.'

'Have.'

'Haven't.'

'Stop,' I said, 'both of you.'

'I never said anything, your honour,' said Mr Kiddington.

'You said "have".'

'No, your honour, he said "haven't".'

'But before that you said "have",' I said.

'Oh, before that. Before that I said a lot of things, your honour. So did you, your honour. So did Mr Benton. So did Mr Jones. So did the clerk, and so did I. But all that was before that, your honour.'

'Have you anything further which you want to ask Mr Jones?' I asked patiently.

'Not if he's rude to me,' said Mr Kiddington.

'Very well then,' I said. 'Mr Benton, is that the case for the plaintiff?'

'It is, your honour,' said Mr Benton.

'Now, Mr Kiddington,' I said, 'would you like to go into the witness box and be sworn and to tell me your story on oath?'

'I haven't any story, your honour,' said Mr Kiddington, 'I can tell you the truth if you'd like to know that.'

'All right,' I said, 'come into the witness box, Mr Kiddington, and tell me the truth.'

The usher thereupon said to Mr Kiddington: 'Take the book in your right hand and repeat the words on the card.'

'I have the book in my right hand,' said Mr Kiddington, 'and here it says: "Swear not at all. Let your communication be Yea, Yea, Nay, Nay; for whatsoever is more than these cometh of evil." Do you know the passage, your honour?'

'Indeed I do,' I said. 'And if I were you Mr Kiddington, I'd read on a bit. "And if any man will sue thee at the law and take away thy coat, let him have thy cloke also." What d'you say to that, Mr Kiddington?'

147

'A hit, a hit, a very palpable hit, your honour,' said Mr Kiddington. 'But what about psalm eighty-nine, your honour: "Justice and judgment are the habitation of thy throne"?'

'If it is against your conscience to swear,' I said, 'you may affirm, Mr Kiddington.'

'I tell you what I'll do, your honour,' said Mr Kiddington, 'I'll promise to do my best to tell the truth.'

'Mr Kiddington,' I asked, 'is that an affirmation binding on your conscience?'

'Of course.'

'Mr Benton, will you be satisfied with that?' I asked.

'Most certainly, your honour.'

'Right, Mr Kiddington,' I said. 'Now tell me what you want to about this.'

'What would you like me to say?' asked Mr Kiddington.

'Tell me your side of the case,' I said.

'How would you like me to put it?' asked Mr Kiddington. 'After all, you're the judge. If I put it the wrong way, you'll decide against me.'

'Tell me why you won't pay the plaintiff's bill.'

'But I've done that already.'

'Tell me again.'

'How many times?'

'Once will do.'

'I won't pay his bill because I didn't get what I ordered.'

'What is wrong with the suit?'

'It isn't to my satisfaction.'

'In what way?'

'In every way. He said he'd make it to my satisfaction, and he hasn't done so. If he'd made it to my satisfaction, I should have paid him. As he hasn't made it to my satisfaction, I won't pay him. Or in other words, I should have paid him if he'd made it to my satisfaction, but I won't pay him as he hasn't made it to my satisfaction. Am I doing all right, your honour?'

'Tell me one thing with which you are not satisfied,' I said.

'One thing?'

'Yes.'

'I'm not satisfied with the suit,' said Mr Kiddington.

'But what doesn't satisfy you about it? I gather he's carried out your instructions about the buttons and the pockets, and the hole in the back of the waistcoat.'

'No,' said Mr Kiddington, 'he didn't make the hole, but I could have made that myself. That's not important. I'd have taken the suit without the hole. After all, I could have cut it out with a pair of scissors, and then I'd have had the bit of cloth as well. Oh no, don't trouble about the hole, your honour. That needn't trouble you at all. After all, if it doesn't trouble me, it needn't trouble you. I wouldn't make a fuss about a little thing like a hole. After all, there are holes and holes. Some holes are terribly important. A well, for example. It's no good having a bad hole if you're digging for a well. It's got to be dug properly. A hole in a wall. That's got to be done properly too, or the wall might collapse. But the hole in the back of a waistcoat, that's a horse of a very different colour. If I may call a hole a horse, your honour. Does anybody mind my calling a hole a horse? Or a horse a hole?'

'Then what is it you complain about?' I asked.

'The whole thing, your honour, it's just not me. If you're a married man, your honour, you'll understand what I mean. You'll take your wife out to buy a dress, and you'll show her something, and she'll say, "That's not me." Well, this suit's not me.'

'But didn't Mr Jones make it as you'd ordered it?'

'Good gracious no, your honour,' said Mr Kiddington, 'I'd have taken it if he'd done that.'

'You'd better carry on, Mr Benton,' I said.

'Mr Kiddington,' said Mr Benton, 'you say you would have paid for the suit if it had been made as you'd ordered it?'

'I said it several times,' said Mr Kiddington, 'but I'll say it again to please you, Mr Benton.'

'Well, in what way was it not as you'd ordered?'

'I've told you,' said Mr Kiddington, 'it wasn't me.'

'Well, wasn't that your fault?' said Mr Benton. 'You told Mr Jones what your requirements were, and if you didn't like the result, that was your responsibility, wasn't it?'

'I didn't make the suit,' said Mr Kiddington.

'No, but it was made according to your instructions. I suggest to you, Mr Kiddington, that you simply changed your mind about it.'

'I never change my mind,' said Mr Kiddington, 'once I've made it up.'

'Perhaps you hadn't made up your mind when you gave the order.'

'If I hadn't made up my mind, I wouldn't have given the order.'

'Ladies sometimes buy dresses and then don't like them when they've got them,' said Mr Benton.

'It wasn't a dress,' said Mr Kiddington, 'it was a suit. And I'm not a lady. Mr Jones guaranteed that I should be satisfied with the suit when he'd made it. I am not satisfied. It's as simple as that.'

'Perhaps you've changed your mind about having a suit at all, Mr Kiddington?'

'Certainly not,' said Mr Kiddington. 'I want a suit. Will your client make me one now?'

Mr Jones could not resist from interrupting from the back of the court: 'I wouldn't make you a suit if I hadn't got any orders at all,' he shouted.

'Silence,' said the usher.

'You see,' said Mr Kiddington, 'he can't do it. I never said it was easy to make me a suit. In point of fact it's very difficult to make me a suit. That is to make a suit that satisfies me. You probably don't believe it, but I'm a very difficult person to satisfy. Actually, I may be a very difficult person altogether. I don't know what you think. I try to behave as well as I can in court, but I've been told that sometimes I'm rather a difficult proposition. Would you call me a difficult proposition, Mr Benton?'

'I'm afraid you mustn't ask me questions, Mr Kiddington,' said Mr Benton.

'That's enough to make anyone difficult,' said Mr Kiddington, 'you can ask me questions, but I can't ask you any. It's much too one-sided. That isn't fair play. But I'll tell you something, Mr Benton. If I were a tailor, I wouldn't accept an order from me. Not if I knew it was me. Because I'd know how difficult a customer I'd taken on. I don't dispute that I'm a difficult customer. If you could satisfy me, you could satisfy anyone.'

'Mr Kiddington,' said Mr Benton, 'I suppose you could pay for the suit if you wanted to?'

'I shall have to think,' said Mr Kiddington.

'Is that why you're defending the case, Mr Kiddington?' I asked. 'Because it would be rather awkward for you at the moment to find twenty-five guineas?'

'I'm still thinking,' said Mr Kiddington.

'If you've got the money,' I said, 'it shouldn't take you all that time to answer, Mr Kiddington. Would it be awkward for you to find twenty-five guineas at the moment?'

'I'm working it out,' said Mr Kiddington.

'It should be simple enough,' I said.

'Not the way I'm working it out,' said Mr Kiddington.

'Oh, come along, Mr Kiddington,' I said, 'you must know the answer by now.'

'This is a court of law,' said Mr Kiddington, 'and I want to be sure that my answer is correct. You'd prefer that, wouldn't you, your honour?'

'Yes, of course,' I said.

'Then I'm afraid I shall have to ask you to wait a moment or two, and I shall need a pencil and paper.'

'If you've got to have a pencil and paper to work it out,' I said, 'it must surely be difficult for you at any rate to find twenty-five guineas. Or at least inconvenient for you to do so. If there were no doubt about it, you could say "yes" straight away.'

'But I don't want to answer in that way, your honour. I've nearly done it now, just wait a moment, please.'

After about half a minute I said: 'Well, Mr Kiddington, I've waited several moments.'

'Your honour shall be rewarded,' said Mr Kiddington. 'I could pay this bill five thousand and four times over. That's why I took a little time, your honour. I didn't want to exaggerate.'

'You've money in the bank, then?' I asked.

'Certainly not,' said Mr Kiddington. 'I don't hold with banks.'

'Then you've stocks or shares?'

'Certainly not.'

'Then what have you got?'

'Well, for one thing, I've got a mansion in the country with about a hundred acres, a swimming pool, a tennis court, and I don't know what else.'

'You own this place, Mr Kiddington?' asked Mr Benton.

'Yes, Mr Benton, I own this place. Anything wrong in that?'

'Is it subject to any mortgage?' I asked.

'Certainly not,' said Mr Kiddington, 'I don't hold with mortgages. Perhaps you'd both like to come and see it.'

There was a slight pause, and then Mr Benton said, perhaps a little meaningfully: 'Tell me, Mr Kiddington, do you employ a lot of people in this mansion of yours?'

'Of course I do. I couldn't run it without.'

'Do any of your employees, by any chance, wear,' Mr Benton paused for a moment, and then added, 'uniforms?'

'Certainly,' said Mr Kiddington.

'I think,' said Mr Benton, 'I think perhaps, your honour, it might be a good thing, if your honour could spare the time, to see Mr Kiddington's mansion.'

'I should be delighted,' said Mr Kiddington. 'Mr Benton too, with pleasure. I could put you both up if you liked, for a weekend perhaps? Or a week there might do you both good.'

'I think you're right, Mr Benton,' I said, 'and that we should accept Mr Kiddington's offer to see his place. If what he says is correct, and he's a wealthy man and could easily pay this bill, it seems to me that the claim should fail. The plaintiff agreed to make a suit to the defendant's satisfaction. That may have been a difficult, or even an impossible thing to do, but the plaintiff agreed to do it. If I'm satisfied that the defendant is honestly not satisfied with the suit, it seems to me he'll succeed in the action. Before I come to that conclusion, however, I ought to know whether it really is the case that Mr Kiddington is the man of means which he says he is.'

'That would be entirely satisfactory from my point of view, your honour,' said Mr Kiddington.

'I don't doubt it, Mr Kiddington,' I said. 'But, if I do decide in your favour for the reasons that I have mentioned, it seems very hard on Mr Jones, who, I suspect, is far from being a wealthy man, that he should have spent his time and labour and money in making a suit, and then should not be paid for it. If what you say is right, Mr Kiddington, you could pay for five thousand such suits. Poor Mr Jones can ill afford to lose the price of one.'

'He shouldn't have taken the order then, your honour,' said Mr Kiddington.

'I'm not talking about the law at the moment, Mr Kiddington. There are other things in life,' I said, 'besides law. Kindness and consideration, for example, play a great part in life. Certainly in a happy life.'

'They should play a great part in everyone's life, your honour,' said Mr Kiddington. 'In your life and in Mr Benton's life. In the usher's life. In the clerk's life. In the postman's life. In the soldier's life. In the First Lord of the Treasury's life. Who's he by the way, your honour?'

'I'm glad you agree with me, Mr Kiddington,' I said, ignoring the question. 'I suggest, then, that we adjourn this case, say, for a week, and during that week Mr Benton and I and Mr Kiddington will inspect the mansion in the country.'

Mr Kiddington then asked if he could question Mr Jones some more before the inspection. I agreed to this, and Mr Jones came back into the witness box.

'Now, Mr Jones,' said Mr Kiddington, 'I've been asked about my means, what about yours? I suggest you're the person short of money, and that's why you're bringing this case.'

'I'm bringing this case,' said Mr Jones, 'because you owe me the money.'

'But suppose I do owe you the money,' said Mr Kiddington, 'is it a good thing for a tailor to sue his customers?'

'It's a good thing for this tailor to sue this customer,' said Mr Jones.

'Is it going to do you any good?' asked Mr Kiddington. 'Let's suppose I do owe you the money. If other people hear about this case, aren't they going to say to themselves "we're not going to a tailor who sues his customers for money"?'

'Look, Mr Kiddington,' said Mr Jones, 'I'm just an ordinary tailor, and, if I do my work properly, I expect to be paid. And I can't afford not to be. If I make a mistake about a suit, I put it right, or take it back. And, if I'm at fault, I stand the loss. But, if I carry out my side of the bargain, I expect the customer to carry out his. Whether the customer owns a mansion in the country, keeps a betting shop, or sweeps the streets. I have to live. And I have to work to live. And I work very hard, I can assure you. I don't like suing people, of course. I don't suppose anybody does, but I did what you asked me to do, and you've got to pay for it. And, if the judge says you haven't, it's not justice, and that's all there is to it. And I don't care who hears me say so.'

'Mr Kiddington,' I said, 'don't you think there's a good deal in what Mr Jones says?'

'Well,' said Mr Kiddington, 'he took long enough over saying it.'

'But don't you think it had some merit?' I asked.

'Everyone's entitled to his own opinions,' said Mr Kiddington.

'If you were the tailor,' I asked, 'and Mr Jones were the customer, wouldn't you agree with what he now says?'

'If I were Mr Jones,' said Mr Kiddington, 'my name wouldn't be Kiddington.'

'Well,' I said, 'but it is Kiddington. Can't you put yourself in Mr Jones' position?'

'I don't want to,' said Mr Kiddington, 'I'm very happy as I am. If I weren't, I shouldn't like to be a tailor.'

'All right,' I said, 'I think we'll adjourn now.'

And so we went down to inspect Mr Kiddington's mansion in the country. And neither Mr Benton nor I were at all surprised to find that, although it did contain everything that Mr Kiddington had said, it was in fact a mental home. I must say that it was beautifully laid out, and it had all the amenities to which Mr Kiddington had referred, and indeed more than those. Eventually we came away. But not before Mr Kiddington had agreed purely as a matter of kindness to pay the whole of Mr Jones' claim, and all his costs, and to let him keep the suit as well.

A day or two later I saw the registrar in my room.

'Charles,' I said, 'I think you might have told me what I was in for.'

'I didn't want to prejudice you,' said the registrar. 'Did he tell you that he owned the place?'

'He did indeed,' I said. 'But *I* can tell *you* something. Not only *did* he own the place, but *he* was the psychiatrist in charge.'

Appendix

Truth or Fiction?

Chapter

1. *Contempt of Court*
   The first part of this story is true. I was held up on the way to court exactly in the way described. But I did not initiate proceedings for Contempt of Court, and all the rest of the story is imaginary, though legally correct.

2. *Free for All*
   Fiction.

3. *Perjury*
   Embellished but based on an actual case.

4. *Chef's Special*
   Fiction.

5. *Retrial*
   Fiction.

6. *The Hidden Money*
   Embellished but based on an actual case.

7. *The Truth*
   Embellished but based on an actual case.

8. *Made to Measure*
   Fiction.

Henry Cecil

According to the Evidence

Alec Morland is on trial for murder. He has tried to remedy the ineffectiveness of the law by taking matters into his own hands. Unfortunately for him, his alleged crime was not committed in immediate defence of others or of himself. In this fascinating murder trial you will not find out until the very end just how the law will interpret his actions. Will his defence be accepted or does a different fate await him?

The Asking Price

Ronald Holbrook is a fifty-seven-year-old bachelor who has lived in the same house for twenty years. Jane Doughty, the daughter of his next-door neighbours, is seventeen. She suddenly decides she is in love with Ronald and wants to marry him. Everyone is amused at first but then events take a disturbingly sinister turn and Ronald finds himself enmeshed in a potentially tragic situation.

'The secret of Mr Cecil's success lies in continuing to do superbly what everyone now knows he can do well.'
The Sunday Times

HENRY CECIL

BROTHERS IN LAW

Roger Thursby, aged twenty-four, is called to the bar. He is young, inexperienced and his love life is complicated. He blunders his way through a succession of comic adventures including his calamitous debut at the bar.

His career takes an upward turn when he is chosen to defend the caddish Alfred Green at the Old Bailey. In this first Roger Thursby novel Henry Cecil satirizes the legal profession with his usual wit and insight.

'Uproariously funny.' *The Times*

'Full of charm and humour. I think it is the best Henry Cecil yet.' P G Wodehouse

HUNT THE SLIPPER

Harriet and Graham have been happily married for twenty years. One day Graham fails to return home and Harriet begins to realise she has been abandoned. This feeling is strengthened when she starts to receive monthly payments from an untraceable source. After five years on her own Harriet begins to see another man and divorces Graham on the grounds of his desertion. Then one evening Harriet returns home to find Graham sitting in a chair, casually reading a book. Her initial relief turns to anger and then to fear when she realises that if Graham's story is true, she may never trust his sanity again. This complex comedy thriller will grip your attention to the very last page.

HENRY CECIL

SOBER AS A JUDGE

Roger Thursby, the hero of *Brothers in Law* and *Friends at Court*, continues his career as a High Court judge. He presides over a series of unusual cases, including a professional debtor and an action about a consignment of oranges which turned to juice before delivery. There is a delightful succession of eccentric witnesses as the reader views proceedings from the Bench.

'The author's gift for brilliant characterisation makes this a book that will delight lawyers and laymen as much as did its predecessors.' *The Daily Telegraph*

THE WANTED MAN

When Norman Partridge moves to Little Bacon, a pretty country village, he proves to be a kind and helpful neighbour and is liked by everyone. Initially it didn't seem to matter that no one knew anything about his past or how he managed to live so comfortably without having to work.

Six months before, John Gladstone, a wealthy bank-robber had escaped from custody. Gradually, however, Partridge's neighbours begin to ask themselves questions. Was it mere coincidence that Norman Partridge had the build and features of the escaped convict? While some villagers are suspicious but reluctant to report their concerns to the police, others decide to take matters into their own hands...

OTHER TITLES BY HENRY CECIL AVAILABLE DIRECT
FROM HOUSE OF STRATUS

Quantity		£	$(US)	$(CAN)	€
	According to the Evidence	6.99	11.50	15.99	11.50
	Alibi for a Judge	6.99	11.50	15.99	11.50
	The Asking Price	6.99	11.50	15.99	11.50
	Brothers in Law	6.99	11.50	15.99	11.50
	The Buttercup Spell	6.99	11.50	15.99	11.50
	Cross Purposes	6.99	11.50	15.99	11.50
	Daughters in Law	6.99	11.50	15.99	11.50
	Fathers in Law	6.99	11.50	15.99	11.50
	Friends at Court	6.99	11.50	15.99	11.50
	Full Circle	6.99	11.50	15.99	11.50
	Hunt the Slipper	6.99	11.50	15.99	11.50
	Independent Witness	6.99	11.50	15.99	11.50
	Much in Evidence	6.99	11.50	15.99	11.50

ALL HOUSE OF STRATUS BOOKS ARE AVAILABLE FROM GOOD BOOKSHOPS OR
DIRECT FROM THE PUBLISHER:

Internet: **www.houseofstratus.com** including author interviews, reviews, features.

Email: **sales@houseofstratus.com** please quote author, title and credit card details.

OTHER TITLES BY HENRY CECIL AVAILABLE DIRECT
FROM HOUSE OF STRATUS

Quantity		£	$(US)	$(CAN)	€
	Natural Causes	6.99	11.50	15.99	11.50
	No Bail for the Judge	6.99	11.50	15.99	11.50
	No Fear or Favour	6.99	11.50	15.99	11.50
	The Painswick Line	6.99	11.50	15.99	11.50
	Portrait of a Judge	6.99	11.50	15.99	11.50
	Settled Out of Court	6.99	11.50	15.99	11.50
	Sober as a Judge	6.99	11.50	15.99	11.50
	Tell you What I'll do	6.99	11.50	15.99	11.50
	Truth With Her Boots On	6.99	11.50	15.99	11.50
	Unlawful Occasions	6.99	11.50	15.99	11.50
	The Wanted Man	6.99	11.50	15.99	11.50
	Ways and Means	6.99	11.50	15.99	11.50
	A Woman Named Anne	6.99	11.50	15.99	11.50

ALL HOUSE OF STRATUS BOOKS ARE AVAILABLE FROM GOOD BOOKSHOPS OR
DIRECT FROM THE PUBLISHER:

Hotline: UK ONLY: **0800 169 1780**, please quote author, title and credit card
details.
INTERNATIONAL: **+44 (0) 20 7494 6400**, please quote author, title,
and credit card details.

Send to: **House of Stratus**
24c Old Burlington Street
London
W1X 1RL
UK

Please allow following carriage costs per ORDER
(For goods up to free carriage limits shown)

	£(Sterling)	$(US)	$(CAN)	€(Euros)
UK	1.95	3.20	4.29	3.00
Europe	2.95	4.99	6.49	5.00
North America	2.95	4.99	6.49	5.00
Rest of World	2.95	5.99	7.75	6.00
Free carriage for goods value over:	50	75	100	75

PLEASE SEND CHEQUE, POSTAL ORDER (STERLING ONLY), EUROCHEQUE, OR INTERNATIONAL MONEY ORDER (PLEASE CIRCLE METHOD OF PAYMENT YOU WISH TO USE) MAKE PAYABLE TO: STRATUS HOLDINGS plc

Order total including postage:_____Please tick currency you wish to use and add total amount of order:

☐ £ (Sterling)　☐ $ (US)　☐ $ (CAN)　☐ € (EUROS)

VISA, MASTERCARD, SWITCH, AMEX, SOLO, JCB:

☐☐☐☐☐☐☐☐☐☐☐☐☐☐☐☐☐☐☐☐☐☐☐☐

Issue number (Switch only):

☐☐☐

Start Date:　　　　　　　　　**Expiry Date:**

☐☐ / ☐☐　　　　　　　　　☐☐ / ☐☐

Signature: _____

NAME: _____

ADDRESS: _____

_____

POSTCODE: _____

Please allow 28 days for delivery.

Prices subject to change without notice.
Please tick box if you do not wish to receive any additional information. ☐

House of Stratus publishes many other titles in this genre; please check our website (**www.houseofstratus.com**) for more details